PRETTY LITTLE TEETH

BOOK 1: A MIDWESTERN HOUSEWIFE NOVELLA

GINA MANAHAN

For Mike

INTRODUCTION

Clarissa
Location: The Little Gray House
Mood: Surprised

"What do you mean, the FBI showed up at your house, Dad? Slow down!"

"Yes! The FBI! G-Men, I think they call them. Can you hear me? Do you have a bad connection on your cell phone? Maybe you should call me on my landline. Cripes. No. They probably bugged that damn thing by now."

I burn the roof of my mouth as I take a too-big swig of piping hot coffee, freshly brewed. Can you blame me? My dad, my sixty-five-year-old loveable dad, tells me he has had the FBI at his house, this very morning.

"Okay. slow down. Tell me what happened."

"I told you! The goddamn FBI showed up at my house and demanded to know where I was on January the sixth."

The FBI? At my dad's house? I honestly wasn't expecting this one. Dad was getting revved up now! I hadn't heard him like this since he found my birth control packets when I was in tenth grade.

"What did you tell them, Dad?" I ask, nervously.

"What do you mean, what did I tell them? The truth, of course! I was sitting my happy ass right here, in my chair, drinking my Diet Coke, and watching TV."

I can hear him, crashing around his bunker and swearing. *No wonder the reception is shit.*

"Okay," I begin.

"Oh, and I also told them that I'm a gun nut, a Trump fan, and a Patriot!" he happily declares.

"Dad! You did not!" I snap.

"Sure did. Then I told those fellas to get on their way and put my taxes to good use."

"Oh, Dad," I groan audibly. I can't help it. It's my midwestern flare of passive aggression.

Two sharp taps on my front door grab my attention.

"Hey, Dad, someone's at the door, I gotta go. Let's talk about this later."

"Sounds good, babycakes. Love you."

My dad clicks off with a chuckle and I know he is in his glory. I have to admit, I felt a little jealous. For as long as I can remember, I have been obsessed with true crime. I would sneak into my parent's bedroom and watch Court TV all summer long when I was eight years old. I was so wrapped up in the OJ case during the fifth grade that I had little time for anything else.

I wanted to be everything from Diane Sawyer to Agent Clarise Starling a la *Silence of the Lambs* when I grew up. And here I am, a basic, thirty-something suburban mom (gag me), with a boring old job as a teacher. What a scam. I would have to get more details from my dad about this later, after he had a chance to go to coffee with the boys, a tradition he upheld every day, except Sunday, when the tiny local coffee shop was closed and they moved the coffee party to church.

I come out of my thoughts to answer the door. *Who is knocking without first calling?* So annoying. I glance out and see the pest truck, emblazoned with the company name: Splinter-O'Neil Extermination – Where We Get The Varmint out of your House, and into your Neighbors.

Complete with a winky face. *God help me.* I hate this new generation of entrepreneurs. They think clever names are so funny. They're not. And by the way, they're bad for business. They could learn a thing or two from my dad. At least he's by himself this time. And I guess he can't help what his dumb-ass boss named the company he works for.

I open the door to a scrawny, pimply-faced twenty-something. He has a ballcap with the company logo pulled down over his beady, dark eyes. His work clothes are rumpled and, honestly, I'm not sure if it's the air that smells, or him.

"I'm here to check the traps," he says, balancing all of his gear on his hip.

I stare at him.

"The mouse traps?" he continues, obviously impatient.

"Oh!" I'm caught off-guard.

Not long ago, my husband was convinced we had mice, and talked about calling this company. But, that was months ago! Surely, Peter would have told me we had mouse traps in our house. Or maybe not. We had honestly been like passing trains lately. Me, on summer break, him, busy at the height of the golf season at the course he ran for our city. There have been crazier things my husband has forgotten to tell me in the last twenty years.

Plus, I'm a sucker for a guy in a uniform. Not necessarily in the romantic way, at least not this one, but a uniform means official and I follow the rules. Most of them. He has a company uniform on, with an official-looking badge, I mean no watermark or anything, but this is a pest control company. How much can I expect? Above the left pocket of his denim work shirt is a company logo, with what looks like a cute little rat but, when I look again, I see it has extra-large fangs and crazy psycho eyes, with the words, *SON Extermination,* below. Oh. I get it. Splinter-O'Neil. Some people really need to check their shit before they open a company.

I sold romance accessories for ten years, so I know this. Can you imagine the innuendos that came up in my marketing? "Now in a Jumbo Size!" could be construed wrong, even though I was selling shaving cream. But really, *SON Extermination*? These people sound like psycho killers, and the extra-nutso type that even attacks their own families.

I stand back, and he shuffles in, carrying a few traps in his hand.

"Thanks," he says. "So I'm just here to check the traps we have installed, check for any signs of mice, you know, the usual," he trails off. I look at him. There is spit, old and new, gathered at the corners of his mouth, that pulls upward on one side, like a grinch sneer, but uglier. His teeth are coated in plaque and Mountain Dew, yellowed and soft-looking.

I look over to where my eight year old, Joseph, is gaming on the couch. He isn't there anymore. *Pew! Pew! Pew!* I hear the familiar sounds coming from his bedroom, at the very back of our sixties walkout ranch. He never has liked strangers, and I take that as a parenting win. This day and age you can never be too careful.

I should know. I'm basically obsessed with anything, true crime, serial killer, or cult-related, and I figure, since I will never actually be Diane Sawyer or Clarise Starling, I can at least imagine that life as long as I can get lost in the pages of any book involving a mystery.

"Ma'am?"

The pest control guy's slippery, wet voice pulls me out of my head. I nod.

"Everything looks good. No shit, no dead mice, no signs of anything. I'm going to leave one trap in your basement furnace area as a precautionary measure, but uh ... yeah. You're good to go. Call us if you have any more pest problems, you hear?"

And even though I didn't know it yet, out walked the pest guy and in walked my very own mystery. My very own, real life experience with a serial killer. Clarise, Diane be damned. This was not work. This was real life.

CHAPTER 1:

NOT BAREFOOT AND PREGNANT

Clarissa
Location: The Little Gray House
Mood: Hot and Cranky

What a weird fucking morning. I've arranged a playdate for Joseph, so I'm able to think. At my own house of course. What? Do you think I'm going to send my kids to someone else's house? Not unless I've checked out their backgrounds and been there myself! Those types of facts are mostly public these days, the important stuff anyway. Do you watch the news? Okay. Then you understand where I'm coming from.

The kids are outside, enjoying the hot summer morning in the sprinkler. It's only 10:00 a.m., and already, it's like *Jurassic Park*: hot, humid, and swamp-assy. Welcome to Minnesota.

My husband, bless him, is at work for what I swear is his millionth hour this week. Now in the winter, I can't get rid of him—he's always around, never gone. The life of two opposite-season workers, I guess. It was actually part of my draw to him, all those years ago. Back when I was all love and marriage and starry-eyed. I thought it would be perfect for a family someday: teacher mom, home with the kids all summer, and dad making us a hot pancake breakfast in the winters when he was off.

Little did I know then that it also meant I would be mom and dad most days, from dawn till dusk, from spring till fall, with winter being our only respite from his schedule. From constantly gone to constantly here, it was a dance we had learned and perfected over the last 20 years. It was exhausting, but I love him and he loves me. Most importantly, he lets me be who I want to be, always, without expectation or conditions. I could look past some scheduling faux pas, especially when I think of who I could have ended up with.

We like to joke that I would be barefoot and pregnant, a stay-at-home mom, and a Republican if I had married any of my ex-boyfriends. I shudder at the thought. My dad probably would have been happy, not for me to not marry Pete or anything, but to have a Catholic, gun-toting Republican for a son-in-law rather than the hippy liberal he had ended up with.

Oh my gosh. Dad! I hope the FBI hasn't come back to arrest him already, because I certainly don't have enough bail money to spring him after my little trip to the medical cannabis pharmacy yesterday. Hey, they were selling weed for 75 percent off, for one day only, and being a mom and a school teacher, I'm a great shopper.

CHAPTER 2:

HIGH FROM THE FBI

Jack Macellaio, Clarissa's dad
Location: Way Far Away, at His House
Mood: High, from Sugar

My damn insulin monitor hasn't stopped going off since I walked in the door. The last thing I need is to hear Ellen squawking about my food choices so early in the morning. I had just been interviewed by the FBI, for chrissakes. Like she hasn't ever emotionally eaten a donut or two.

I can feel the sickly sweet frosting on my teeth. I savor it, like a kitten with a bowl of cream. My sugar is already at 300. May as well get as much sugar in as I can before I clean up my diet tomorrow. I have to see my diabetes doctor next week. The prices of my medications have skyrocketed, because apparently they are all the rage to lose weight or something. Anyway, I have to skimp a little bit now that the prices have quadrupled, so I really shouldn't be doing this.

"Can you believe?" I yelled at coffee this morning. "The literal FBI!"

I mean, I'm a Patriot, of course! But who isn't? I'll tell you who, the Democrats! And they are ruining this country. I tell my daughter this every day. The liberal, Democrat one, Clarissa. Can you believe it? She's a public school teacher and, I hate to say it, but public schools are exactly what is wrong with this country. Taking prayer out of school and what not. I said this to my daughter one time, and can you believe what she said? She says, "Dad," she says to me. "Whose religion?"

Whose religion? The Catholic religion of course! I don't even answer her anymore when she says those silly things. I am much older than her and much wiser. I think she got brainwashed at that state college. And I'm not going to outright say it, but do you think she teaches at a Catholic school? One of my other daughters? She went to a Catholic college. And you can guess what happened. She's still Catholic, she's still Republican, and she agrees with me! None of this progressive left-wing bullshit for her!

I love all my kids equally, and I mean that with all my heart. My mom had ten, and she handled that much better than women these days and most of them only have one or two. I just don't know what went wrong with Clarissa. That's why I'm pretty sure it was that state school she went to. That's exactly what happens when you take religion out of schools, just like I always say.

CHAPTER 3:

TATER TOT HOTDISH

Leroy
Location: Leroy's Dirty Work Truck
Mood: Deflated

It was almost lunchtime, and I couldn't wait to get home for my forty-five-minute break. My babies needed to be fed, and I had scooped up some fresh little baby frogs they liked so much from the creek. They didn't like them right away, not typical rat food, but when that's all I feed them, they take what they can get and now they prefer it. I love watching them tear the little legs off the froglets. It's kind of like humans: Adapt, evolve, mutate.

My mom was making tater tot hotdish . . . oh my God, I'm salivating. *Bitch better crisp up them tots how I like or—*

Or what? I'll move out? I laugh at the thought. *Yeah, right. That old bird will be gone soon enough.* At eighty-five, I'm sure of it. And if that's not what nature has in mind? Well. I chuckle. I can cross that bridge if it comes.

I turned down the gravel side road that led to the trailer park where I live with my mom and pet rats. Grew up here at Paradise Park, seems like forever ago, with my mom, my sister, and my dad. Not much has changed, except the prices. Keep going up and people have to keep moving out. *Paradise Park.*

I snort at the thought of whoever named this trash heap any sort of paradise or a park. There is nothing happy here, or any swings, slides, or even a puny sandbox. *Oh well. Better to have less kiddies round these parts.* Too many drug dealers, perverts, and, well, people like me, if I'm being honest. I can't help it. I'm just like my daddy and his daddy before him.

I thought back to that little gray house on the hill I had just come from. Now was she a looker! I look down at my lap and see my wimpy erection. *Bitch.*

CHAPTER 4:

TEA TiME

Clarissa

Location: The Little Gray House on the Hill, the Deck

Mood: High (Medically)

I grab my vape and head to the deck to call my dad. Cannabis will make this much easier. God bless the USA, I guess. My dad thinks I'm so unpatriotic, but hey, finally, a thing we got right! Lavender Laze, my prescription says. It is known for its sweet lavender flavor that activates on the exhale. Lots of good terpenes and all that. I don't know. I'm not fancy and I may not understand all their hip language down at the dispensary, but what I do know is that this is very fancy stuff.

I call my dad's cell. No answer. Typical. He was the first to have a bag phone in 1988, but just can't seem to keep track of his cell phone once we finally convinced him to get one. Don't even bring up texting. Not happening. Secretly, he had confided in me that he definitely knows how to get texts and operate texting, it just wasn't his thing and he didn't like people invading his time, and I get that. I'm totally open to texts any time of the day, but you better not text me again demanding that I respond, or send me question marks, even worse. For all you know, I could be writing the next Great American Novel or something.

I could call the house, but Ellen and I would probably get into some long discussion about something, as we always do, and I'm in the mood for short and sweet. I blow smoke rings with my vape as my muscles unwind. *How is my family related?* I wonder. *We are all so different.*

My cell phone rings and *June* flashes on the caller ID. What fresh hell is this? Although I talk to my mom daily, I always call her, not the other way around. One time, I actually did an experiment where I didn't call her for eight weeks, just to see what happened. When I finally broke down and called her, because what girl doesn't ultimately want her mom, you'll never guess what she said. No, I swear, you won't.

She said, "Hi, honey! How's the weather?" as if the last fucking eight weeks of blankness didn't happen. That was the moment I realized that I needed my mom more than she wanted me, and I'm still working on swallowing that dry-ass pill.

"Hello, Mom?" I say, picking up my phone.

"Clarissa? Is that you?" she yells.

"Yeah, it's me, Mom, you don't have to yell." The phone sounds crackly. She doesn't always have the best service at the commune where she lives. She sounded offended when I asked her if it was a nudie commune when she first moved in. Wouldn't that be your first question? Anyway, she assured me that it's "just a group of like-minded people, living off the grid together."

I'm sorry, but I also know a lot about cults. I actually joined one for a decade once, which is a whole other story, but yeah. I know from reading, watching, and being in one that isolating people away from others is the number one *modus operandi* of any cult. I don't think the commune has any one idolized leader (yet), but I have a conspiracy theory I am tossing around that involves social media.

"What?" she yells. "I'm having a hard time hearing you! I'm calling because I heard from Suzie's cousin's nephew, Frank, that the FBI was at your father's house this morning."

"Oh," I said. Of course. Le sigh. My mom wants information. Classic motivation for her to initiate a phone call. Well, I can play that game too, as I am her daughter, after all.

"Huh, I haven't heard a thing," I lied.

And although I could hear the disappointment in my mom's voice, I could also hear the giddiness of her barely contained excitement, for she knew something first, before me. I wondered how many Hail Marys that lie ought to cost me. *None. God would understand. He might even be thanking me for keeping a little peace on earth.*

I lay back on my patio chair, the one on my deck oasis, where absolutely no one can see me but I can see them, and I sample some more Lavender Laze. Why hasn't anyone started selling weed-flights yet? With an iced-coffee flight, the ones that are all the rage right now? Can you imagine? Three mini-dog walker joints, starting off with a sativa, moving to a hybrid, and finishing it off with an indica? Paired with an adorable mini iced coffee flight, preferably one crème brûlée, one hazelnut, and one banana nut, with homemade whip and sprinkles on top. Cinnamon on the banana nut, of course, just a little dusting, like my favorite cafe.

With that, I take a last hit of my Lavender Laze vape and feel my tummy growl. *Ahh, yes.* Definitely a couch-melter indica, I take a few minutes to stretch my now pleasantly un-tense neck as I curl up in the chair and shut my eyes. *Damn PTSD.*

CHAPTER 5:

i SAW YOU

Molly, Clarissa's stalker
Location: Molly's Horrid Brain
Mood: Intrigued

I remember the first day I saw you. We were at school on a late fall afternoon, meeting the kids' teachers after the first few weeks were finished. The leaves were orange-red, about to fall, the perfect ripeness of autumn leaves in the midwest. You walked, or rather ran, into the gymnasium, right as the presentation started. You were clearly late: harried and anxious. You had a little blonde kid in tow. Must be yours, you look identical. I'll never forget those matching deep brown eyes.

I saw everything in you that I so badly wanted in myself.

You smiled at me.

God, that smile. It made me feel so welcome.

"Is this seat taken?" you asked.

"Not for you!" I answered, wiping my sweaty palms on my lap. "Have a seat!"

CHAPTER 6:

SOGGY TOTS

Leroy
Location: Leroy and Marge's House
Mood: Powerful

I gobble up my tater tot hotdish faster than my mom can slop it on my plate. Greasy hamburger meat from the discount bin, a can of corn, cream of mushroom soup, and crispy tater tots spell heaven. I always like it best when she makes those little fluffy crescent rolls to go with it. I love to sop up the juices from the hotdish, making the crescent roll warm and wet. I giggle. *Warm and wet. Just the way I like my bitches.* If I had any bitches, that was. Or even just one bitch. Women. Useless. The whole lot of them, starting with my mother.

In our house, hot dish rotation made the eating cheap and the cooking easy, two necessities. Plus, Mom needs mushy food and I'm not blending shit up for her, so we settled on hotdish. Depending on what's on sale or what I kill in the woods, we eat pretty good with a decent variety. Tater tot hotdish. Venison hotdish. Sunday dinner hotdish. Lutheran funeral hotdish. Pizza hotdish. Chicken pot pie hotdish. Goulash hotdish. Rabbit hotdish. Endless options.

"Leroy! Listen to me!" Mom sputtered. Her sickly, old-lady spit was landing on my face with every word. "I said your sister called."

"What does that bitch want?"

"Well, to speak with her brother, for one. For two, she said you ain't paid the rent over at her place for two months and they're about to kick her out."

"Bout fucking time," I say with my mouth full of hotdish.

"What? Speak up, Leroy! I can't hear you when you mumble! You know I need hearing aids!"

I set my fork down, calmly. Then I wipe my face off, leaving a trail of meat, gravy and corn down the left side of my mouth. No one interrupts my lunch. Especially griping about shit we can't afford. Plus I like when the old lady is half deaf. Makes living with her easier.

"Mother," I say calmly. "Come here."

As soon as she enters my space, I backhand her across the face, sending her glasses, dentures, and her flying into the bookshelves lining the dining room, where I keep my rat supplies and Mom keeps her porcelain doll collection.

Marge

I lay on the floor, curled up, silent, pretending to be dead so that he might leave me alone. He likes hurting me and it isn't as fun for him if I'm quiet. He is my son, after all. I know him like the back of my hand, even if I don't like him.

The old cuckoo clock pops out and chimes the time. Leroy's lunch break is over. All I need to do is wait, stay quiet, stay still, and he would be gone. I feel my gummy mouth with my tongue. *That sick boy. Always knocking teeth out.* My dolls are scattered about the floor, eyelashes sticking to the porcelain, leaving some of them staring at me with one eye open.

A shadow looms over me. Big, black musty boots, stinking of feet and rat poop, block my vision.

"Next time, make the tots crispy, how I like 'em."

And he spits on me.

CHAPTER 7:

RAT-FACE

Jack
Location: Way Far Away
Mood: Suspicious

"And where did you say you were on January sixth?" the skinny, rat-faced one asks me, as I'm being formally interrogated.

"As I've said before, I have no clue what I was doing two and a half years ago, but surely not what you're accusing me of."

"And what's that, sir?" Old Rat-Face again.

"Well! You're the copper, aren't ya? Whatever it is that made you drive all the way here to ask little-old me, who has never been east of Chicago, if I was part of that mess at the Capitol."

"What's your business in Chicago?" chirps the bald, fat one.

"Business? I have family in Chicago, Sir!" Jack spat angrily.

"Ah, yes! Family!" Rat-Face smirks. He looks like a damn rat with a whole room full of cheese. I swear he clicks his teeth at me as he lays down a glossy eight-by-ten photo.

"And can you identify this individual, Jack?" Rat-Face asks.

"Why do you have a picture of my cousin Johnny? What is this?!"

"Now can you tell me what year you got rid of your refrigerated van, Mr. Macellaio? This one?" He slides another photo on the table. *A photo of my damn ham van!*

"Now this is ridiculous! I haven't had that van for the better part of two decades! That ham van was the first of its kind, really! Cold enough to drive hams all the way to Chicago and back!"

Rat-Face snatches his glossy photos back up, returns them to his important-looking leather document folder, and stands up. Baldy follows his lead.

"Mr. Macellaio, I would advise you not to leave town. We will be in contact."

And they walk down the narrow footpath, past the statue of the Virgin Mary in the garden, and continue in their fancy suits down the dusty alley on foot.

Where the fuck did those goons leave their car?

"And keep your hands off my blueberry bushes! I'll know!" Jack yelled. There. No blueberries for them.

CHAPTER 8:

OFF-GRID iPAD

Clarissa

Location: In my memories

Mood: Cynical

My mom and her domestic partner, Sheep, live off the grid, in the middle of nowhere. That's what my mom tells people when they ask her where she's from. "Oh you know, the middle of nowhere!" she says, and she explodes laughing every single time. I'm not sure how she can still think that shit is funny, because it wasn't funny even the first time, but back to the *Let's Meet June Show*!

My mom and Sheep pride themselves on living away from civilization and all the things, like you get an award for it or something. They got super-obsessed with the show, *Tiny House Hunters* a while back. You know that show? Guess what? People like my mom, or really anyone, should wonder why they don't have a show called *Tiny Houses, Where Are They Now?* Because guess what? They can't make that show about anyone who stayed long-term in a tiny house, because they aren't in a tiny house anymore. I'm sure of it.

Sheep is bald, and has been since I met him twenty-five years ago. I wasn't sure how to ask him for a while why he was called Sheep, since he was in fact bald. Finally I got over my nerves, because, clearly, I couldn't be the first person that had asked. It's quite odd to have a nickname of a furry animal when you are bald. So, Sheep told me that he used to have "gorgeous, flowing, curls." His words, not mine. Apparently the girls loved it. But, he was never married or seriously dated before he met my mom at forty, so apparently they didn't love it that much.

Shortly after the *Commune Announcement* as I've begun calling it, Sheep decided that he was going to also go back to the ways of the past, and got himself a wig. And it's not a good wig. I think it came from the Internet, not made for him or anything, and it always sits just a titch crooked. I want to reach out and fix it, but then I would have to touch him, and Sheep and I are just not like that. We have a no-touching relationship. This is overridden only at significant life events, such as funerals. Not birthday parties. Significant. Anyway, Sheep is bald underneath, but he wears a super thick, curly beige wig that reminds me of a cross between a goldendoodle and a bichon perched atop his head. Sheep is kind of my step-dad, or I guess my mom's life partner, depending on the day and how they are defining things. I get that. I'm not big on definitions, either. Sheep is open to whatever my mom has in mind, so I wasn't shocked that he easily agreed to move to the commune.

I hope you understand June and Sheep better, because they are still quite a mystery to me. Take this, for example: Even though my mom prides herself on living like the foragers before us, let me tell you a dirty little secret: She has an iPad. Not only does she have an iPad, she's addicted to it. She literally uses it constantly, even when she's around actual humans, which is a rarity, and you would think, wouldn't you, that she would want to interact with humans once and a while? But apparently the old social media newsfeed is way more interesting.

One thing that makes me pee myself laughing every time I remember it is that my mom doesn't even have a real toilet. She has a composting porta potty or some shit. And trust me, if anyone should own a real, proper, flushing toilet, it's my mother. But she charges the iPad somehow, right? Solar power.

I am not kidding you. Come hell or high water, out in the lands they forage, my mom finds sun. For if there is no sun, there is no Internet, and if there is no Internet, then there is no social media. And if there is no social media then, surely, surely, the world would end.

CHAPTER 9:

i SAT WiTH YOU

Molly
Location: The Elementary School
Mood: Stalkerish

YOU SIT NEXT TO ME IN AN OLD RICKETY METAL CHAIR IN THE GYMNASIUM of our kids' school. You have a bead of sweat running from your temple to your jawbone. It's the first thing I see, actually. I want to taste it.

You unload your bag, the one with the cutsie daisy print (I want one!!!), get your son settled, and mouth, *Thank you!* to me as we listen to the principal drone on about stupid shit. I have way more important things to do, ugh! Like finding that daisy-print bag. I wonder which of your favorite stores you bought it at. I wonder what your favorite stores are. I have so much to learn about you.

But, it's okay, because I'm with you, and you are with me. I let out a contented sigh, perhaps too loudly. I'm a little awkward, okay? I'm working on it. But, to my dismay, you don't seem to think I'm weird! You look over, smile at me, and look back at the principal, to listen.

Clarissa . . . I say your name over and over in my mind. I like how it feels. I can't wait to say it out loud. I can't wait to say your name to you, and you acknowledge me. Oh . . . I can't wait.

CHAPTER 10:

ME AND MOLLY

Leroy

Location: Leroy's Dirty Work Truck

Mood: Madder than a Wet Cat

I'M MADDER THAN A WET ALLEYCAT AS I DRIVE BACK TO WORK. NEVER MIND my bitch mother, but now my bitch sister? It's too much for one day, it really is.

Ahhhh, Molly. The real nutter of the family. A real piece of work, that one. Her special talent is looking and sounding totally normal. She's anything but normal, trust me. Ask her old boyfriends, friends, doctors, therapists, teachers. They know. You think I'm vicious? Meet my older sister, who's taught me everything I know.

The really sad part is that Molly has no friends and no life, because people figure out real quick-like what a weirdo she is. She globs onto them, like butter on corn, and suffocates them. That's what I think anyway. She's the obsessive type, a real stage-nine clinger.

I'm not sure what she does all day, but work is not one of them, and so she mooches off of me just like her bitch mother. She doesn't really have time for a job with all the watching she does. The ones she's had, she's been fired from.

I could cut her off anytime, I suppose, but Molly and her craziness usually come in handy from time to time. I'll pay her rent for the next six months, I decide, as I pull into work at *SON Extermination*. Then, I'll have the upper hand again. It's one thing Molly and I constantly fight each other for, wordlessly. Power and control. She's more into manipulation, I use domination and fear. And pain. Same result. Cut from the same cloth.

This will work out nicely, I decide. By damn, I'm whistling!

CHAPTER 11:

THE ONE THAT DIDN'T GET AWAY

Marge
Narrator: Marge's Memories
Mood: Reminiscent

IT HASN'T ALWAYS BEEN THIS WAY. ME STUCK HERE, I MEAN. BOTH LEROY and his sister have gotten meaner with age, just like their daddy. I blame him. Mean old man. I blame the drugs he did before he dropped his seed in me, I blame the way he beat me in front of those kids. Oh, I blame him for everything.

He's dead now. Good riddance is what I say about that. I thought things would be better with him gone, but I was wrong. As soon as my husband died, Leroy went crazier than my husband ever was. And I haven't left this house since.

Only Leroy lives here with me now, even he wouldn't be stupid enough to have all of us live under one roof. Someone, or two someones, would end up dead. His crazy sister—my crazy daughter—lives five miles away from me and thankfully has no car. I like that. Keep the crazies separate.

Which always makes me wonder. If my husband was crazy, and my kids are both crazy, does that mean I'm crazy, too?

CHAPTER 12:

THE CASE OF THE MISSING BIC

Clarissa

Location: The Deck at the Little Gray House
Mood: Uneasy

I WAKE UP AT 5:30, AS USUAL, BEFORE THE SUN, MY CHILD, MY KITTY CAT, and the world. *Pee or coffee?* . . . my never-ending internal dialogue in the morning. I should, in fact, start with water and exercise like a normal suburban housewife, but I've never been normal, and I don't much like suburbia. I prefer coffee, cigarettes, and a side of weed. What? It's medicinal, and legal for me, and it's summer break. I'm not working. Don't be jealous.

I take my coffee in my favorite chipped mug from the Lazy Loon to the patio. Best gift shop in Minnesota, the Lazy Loon. As the caffeine hits my bloodstream, I can feel myself waking up. Remembering the craziness of the past few days, I laugh at the thought of my dad being interviewed by FBI agents. I bet he gave it right back to them. My dad is passionate about his politics and "The State of America," but he's no criminal.

I reach for my pink glitter Bic lighter, the one that I suppose makes me feel like less of a dirtball for sneaking weed and cigarettes so early in the morning, but it's not there.

I know what you're thinking: It's just a lighter, and you seem to smoke like a chimney, so you probably moved it, or someone else used it, or there is some other perfectly rational explanation. But no. You're wrong. My deck doesn't have stairs to it and it's thirty feet in the air, at the top of a hill. There's no way anyone can access this deck from the outside, unless you happen to have a bucket truck or a helicopter, in which case, I would hear something long before anyone snagged my glitter Bic. So no. They didn't come from the deck.

I try to ignore my memory of using it right before I went to bed last night, but my every-woman-in-America senses are tingling. Something is not right. If anything, I lay traps for thieves, specifically my husband, the only thief with access and motivation in the last twelve hours. But he didn't have an opportunity. Pete was still sleeping, and because my husband has a habit of pilfering my fire, I bought the glitter Bic as a preventive measure. He hates the look and feel of glitter so much that he literally cannot touch it. *And people think moms do nothing. Look at how much effort I have to put into just keeping my stuff out of everyone else's mitts. Let's not even get started on the millions of meals and snacks I have made in the last eight years.*

There is also no way I am wrong about this, because I'm obsessed with all things true crime, and I know, I just know, that something is wrong.

CHAPTER 13:

ALL GOOD CATHOLICS

Jack

Location: In Jack's Memories

Mood: Thankful for not Choking on my Porkchop

WAIT UNTIL PETEY HEARS ABOUT THIS ONE, I THINK TO MYSELF. HE LOVES a good story, old Pete! It hadn't always been this way between us. *Hah! It had been anything but, in fact!*

But let me ask you this. Say your daughter comes to you and she says, "Dad, my boyfriend likes the whiskey too much!" I'm sure you would give him a hard time, too, and boy did I! Oh, ho, I did. But, Pete redeemed himself, and he takes good care of my daughter and his son, and has cleverly switched to vodka. Much more responsible. A good decision. Even better, he's such an involved dad that he doesn't even drink the vodka. He sticks to water, usually, unless my daughter makes him mad, which I can 100 percent understand. Used brandy raising that one, I did. Couple of fingers of brandy and a couple of ice cubes for me, a good movie, and a cozy chair. Worked every time, and Clarissa was always calmed down and was on to her next thing by the time my movie was over. I'm glad Pete had seen the light.

Over the years we've gotten closer, me and Pete. Oh, not as close as my other sons-in-law. But, in their defense, they are hunters and patriots and Republicans! And, they go to church, the Holy Catholic Church. Now. I'm not saying Pete doesn't take his family to church, because how would I know, and that's between him and God anyway. But, the last time we prayed at dinner as a family, you know, the prayer before you eat that starts, "Bless us, O Lord?" Well, it got to the part where you say, *Through Christ, our Lord, Amen*, right there at the very end? Well, Petey, he says, *For thine is the kingdom, the power and the glory, now and forever.*

Damn near choked on my porkchop. Any good Catholic knows that the part Pete said is the "Our Father" not the "Bless us, O Lord!" But, anyway, that's probably what happens when you take prayer out of school. *Wait, didn't Peter actually go to Catholic school?*

CHAPTER 14:

i STALKED YOU

Molly

Location: Molly's Apartment and Sick Mind

Mood: Minnesota Nice

I'm scrolling through your social media. I'm back to 2008, before you had a baby, before you had two miscarriages, before you paid a shit ton of money to have a test tube baby . . . *Gross!* I'm sorry your parts don't work like a real woman's should. With the list of bad habits I'm seeing, I have an idea why.

You can learn a lot from social media! Even from someone like you, who has most of it locked down. I can see enough. I like what I see. You're kind, funny, witty, and confident. You're smart, sassy, and fun. Everyone loves you. And coffee. Boy, are you obsessed! You should probably work on that. It's kind of a gross habit and is probably why you're looking a little chunkier than you did in your older online pictures. It's okay, I like you both ways! Does Pete, though? You know how men are.

Born in 1983. Grew up in a tiny town in the middle of nowhere. Moved to college in Fargo in 2003, I'm guessing to get away from the boyfriend who broke your heart around that time. I'm just guessing, but I bet I'm right. I'm definitely starting to know you better. Moved to the Big City for your first teaching job in 2006, hopefully before you picked up that disgusting Fargo accent. Yuck.

You met your husband in 2006, too. Can you say codependent much? Sorry, but it's true. I would know. I totally get it.

Then comes miscarriage, miscarriage, and finally your precious alien baby in 2015. I mean, your dad can't be okay with that, can he? That's not very Catholic, test tube babies. "Begotten, not made" from the Nicene Creed? Isn't that what it means? No making babies in tubes? I don't know. I'm not Catholic.

I never did understand baby obsessions. Babies are so . . . I don't know. Leechy. Like what do they do for you? Nothing, except take, and I hate people like that. I don't care if they are babies or not. Horrible trait.

That takes us to 2023, when we met, or rather, will meet. Officially.

I like most of what I'm seeing, but some of this? Clarissa! If we are going to be best friends, you have some work to do. I cannot be best friends with someone who does some of the dumb things you do. I have a list of things for you to get started on.

You're husband is pretty hot, from what I've seen. And it looks like he should be pretty easy to find.

CHAPTER 15:

SERiAL KiLLERS AND BARBiE DOLLS

Clarissa

Location: In my Memories

Mood: Reflective

WHILE MOST GIRLS MY AGE WERE PLAYING WITH BARBIE DOLLS, PAINTING their nails, and having lemonade stands, I was sniffing out true crime and other unsavory stories around my neighborhood and beyond, since the age of eight when I first stumbled upon channel twenty-one, Court TV. Court TV blossomed into *Unsolved Mysteries*, *Rescue 911*, *Dateline, 20/20, Nancy Grace,* and every other crime show I could get my hands on.

Now, in the age of streaming documentaries, I have a plethora of options at my fingertips. Name a cult, serial killer, or otherwise interesting crime in the last seventy-five years, and I'll provide you a short bio.

I love shows that explore the inner psyche. I don't believe people are born evil, I really don't. After all the true crime I've devoured, I know better. We make our own monsters. I'm currently watching, *Signs of a Psychopath* on Hulu. I highly recommend it if you want to brush up on your serial killer-dodging skills.

I should know. I'm a school teacher. Do you think I do this for the glory or the pay? No. It's because I care about humanity, even though that's not what the media currently wants you to think. *Just another loser teacher.* Exhausting. No. I see every day that every human has a story, and I also see the barriers that are unfair, unequal, and rampant in our country.

More than a lot of people, I think, I can understand people's wrongdoings. It doesn't mean I support them, but I absolutely can understand them. Probably because I've had lots of them myself. But haven't we all? When you take the time to look under all of the layers, I think you will find that no one ever wanted to be a bad person. But sometimes that's what people turn into, because of the millions of problems in our country. And it's not taking religion out of school, like my dad likes to tell me every morning at 5:30. I don't have the answer, but that's why I go to work every single day, because I do think there is a quantifiable, although complicated and complex, answer and that we can do better for our world by making our schools a better place for everyone. That, and I have friends there, and I actually love work, believe it or not. Summer gets long. Plus, it's right down the street from my favorite coffee place, extra bonus.

I don't go to church, or do all of the fancy organized religion stuff, but I do believe in being a good person, and I'm pretty sure Jesus hung out with the lepers and the prostitutes, so I think I'm on the right track. We shouldn't be running away from those who are different from us, or think differently than we think, we should be running toward them . . . or something. Anyway, I'm just a high school teacher, but I hope by retirement, at eighty-eight, when my pension is supposedly ready, I hope I can say I have made an impact.

I just try to be nice to everyone I meet. Keep it simple. Whether it's a smile, or a "Hi!" I think just noticing people goes a long way for the world. The problem is, I seem to have a habit of saying "Hi!" or smiling at the wrong ones. And you never know who the wrong ones are until it's way too late. Serial Killer 101.

CHAPTER 16:

DON'T F WiTH MY COFFEE

Clarissa

Location: In my Memories

Mood: High Maintenance

WHENEVER I GO VISIT MY FAMILY, WHICH ISN'T OFTEN, I SHACK UP WITH my parents. What? I'm a teacher, and the hotels charge a minimum of 200 bucks a night, anywhere in town, especially during the summer. Which I completely don't understand, because I can get a room in downtown Minneapolis for less, at a nicer place with a view, and without a stinky fish-cleaning shack in the parking lot. I try to alternate parent stays just like they did with weekends so no one gets mad, but that's impossible. I usually stay at whichever is more convenient for our plans and deal with the aftermath from the other parent.

So, anyway, this time, I was staying with my mom and Sheep and trying their accommodations on for size. It was just me and Joseph, Pete could hardly ever come with us because he worked so much and I didn't make the trip in the winter too often, especially alone. The roads up there were tiny, little twisty things, ice-lined and surrounded by deer just waiting to pop out at you and ruin your night. Or possibly kill you

Honest to God, people up there have special things on the front of their car so that deer don't do so much damage. They're called grill guards, I think, look it up if you don't believe me. You're going to think I'm lying, but I am not. They also sell deer whistles, smart little ultrasonic devices you can mount to your car! Honest to God. I guess while you're driving, the whistle emits a noise only deer can hear, and apparently they don't like it and you won't hit a deer if you get one. I wonder if I can get one to strap on my car just for those trips.

It's 4:30 a.m. as this was back when Joseph was a baby and got up religiously at 5:00 a.m. every day. So, I got smart and I started getting up before him and making sure I had some coffee in me before something besides my Netflix and bladder needed attention.

I had brought my own coffee beans, because I am kind of a coffee snob. Not as bad back then as I am now, but a snob nonetheless. I didn't want to be a rude houseguest, especially when I'm staying here for free, you know? So when I got up I was ready to have some piping-hot medium roast, with the bottled water I brought to brew it with, because let's not even get started on the water up there. Stinky. Perfectly healthy, but definitely an acquired taste.

So I'm ready to make my coffee, and I see that my mom has already made it. That was nice! It's so nice to have someone do something for me once in a while! My mom poured the coffee into the cup and I took one look at it and made a face. I didn't mean to, it just happened. And it was a nasty face. A, what the fuck is this and how in the world would you expect me, of all people, to drink that?

"What, Clarissa?" my mom said. "I see that ugly face you're making. What's the problem with the coffee this time?"

I decide I'm going to go for it, because I'm stuck here for three days and I can't live that long without proper coffee. My mom wasn't living off the grid yet, but she lived way out in the middle of nowhere and the closest coffee was an hour away. They do have an amazing coffee shop, I make sure to visit all the time. I buy coffee, artwork, and books there because they sell it all. Now, they don't sell true crime books, which would make it a home run for me, but it's pretty close and locally owned.

"Where do I start with what's wrong with it, Mom? Look at it. Looks like piss water. Why is it that color?"

"Oh my God, Clarissa. There is nothing wrong with this coffee. It is perfectly fine. I used the grounds from yesterday and, let me tell you, that was some good coffee."

"Mom," I say. "You reused the grounds from yesterday?"

"Correct," she says smugly.

"You didn't use the special coffee I brought for us, or the special water from The Big City?"

"Correct. This is not a hotel, missy! You should be thankful I got up early and made this for you. My circadian rhythm is not used to this. I prefer to get up later and snuggle with Sheep as long as I can in the morning. And you are so loud, you and your elephant-stomping feet."

Oh. My. God. Please help me keep my face from showing how I really feel.

I try to be gracious, because she's right, this isn't a hotel and she is getting old, so she probably does need to sleep longer. I have been telling people forever that sleep prevents dementia and Alzheimer's, so this whole hustle culture has got to go. One of my old bosses hated it when I told him this. But you know what? He has a whole lot more gray hair than is normal for a man his age and should sleep more . . . Maybe my mom is a casualty from all her hard work, too.

"Okay, Mom, you're right. I'm sorry," I say. "Can you get the hazel-nut creamer?"

My mom had insisted on going shopping for us, to get things to make us feel comfortable and welcome. I'm a bring-my-own kind of gal, but if she was offering, I wasn't turning it down. The last time my mom had footed the bill for my groceries was when I first moved to college and she stocked me up on ramen noodles, kiwi-strawberry Shasta, rice, and salsa at the Local

CA$H-WI$E. This time, I made sure to add some things I could take home, too. I wondered if she would notice I had added really nice toilet paper to the list. The big pack, the kind rich people buy. *Or probably at least principals.*

She hands me a bottle of French vanilla creamer.

"Oh, sorry Mom, this is vanilla. I think you grabbed the wrong one. Hit me with the hazelnut!"

"Oh, no, Clarissa, that isn't a mistake. Your dad is right. You need a good, long confession and you also need to be taught a lesson," my mom lectures me. "Hazelnuts are disgusting and French vanilla is way better. Like I've mentioned plenty of times before, this isn't a hotel. I didn't think it was very funny that you put toilet paper on the list. Especially a 100 pack. We're retired, Clarissa, and we live on a fixed income."

I roll my eyes, thinking of the $200,000 camper they bought last year.

Internally, I was fuming. I waited for my mom to go back to bed, to cuddle with Sheared Sheep (my angry name for him), and I made myself a pot with my special beans and special water. And I stood over that coffee pot until the last drop was brewed, lest she fuck with it.

Then, I grabbed ten bucks out of her purse and drove to the grocery store an hour away to get my own hazelnut creamer.

CHAPTER 17:

PEACHES AND PANSIES

Leroy
Location: Little Gray House
Mood: Pervy

"G'morning," I say.

The morning is hot and muggy already. I'm hit with a blast of cold air as she opens the door. It feels amazing. Her nightgown is clinging to her round tits that look like ripe little peaches. It's white and gauzy, with tiny little flowers on it.

I choke on my spit a little bit as I get a glimpse of her hard nipples. "Good morning, um, missus." She's uncomfortable, I can tell. Wondering why I'm here again. "Wanted to check on them traps," I say.

"I thought you said we were all good last time you were here," she asks, confused.

"Oh, you are, and I did, ma'am. But, you see, here at *Splinter O-Neil Extermination*, we believe in good customer service, as much as we care about killing a few rodents, you know?"

"Um, yeah . . . . Soo . . . " she stumbles over her words.

Pretty little thing is speechless, just how I like them. Put out or shut up, you know? And this bitch clearly ain't putting out for me. Yet.

I wonder what her husband has that I don't.

I've seen his little pansy ass at the golf course he works at. Real piece of work, that one. Probably has a few bitches on the side, from what I've seen. Women are all over him. Hugging him, rubbing his forearm, basically getting it on right there in public. I will never understand women, ever. Meanwhile, I can't get a goddamn one to look at me, let alone have sex with me. Useless. All of them.

"So about them traps? In the laundry room?" I repeat.

I can tell she doesn't want to let me in. She gives it away in the change in her face, the change in her physical presence. She has her arms crossed over her chest now, making herself smaller, trying to make me unsee her tits. *Good luck.* I smile at her, my yellowed teeth making her even more uncomfortable.

"I'll just be a moment, ma'am." I reassure her. *Always reassure your prey. They'll be less skittish that way.*

CHAPTER 18:

I PRETENDED TO BE YOU

Molly

Location: The Coffee Shop and the Golf Course
Mood: Thirsty

I PULL INTO YOUR FAVORITE COFFEE SHOP WITH YOUR GO-TO ORDER MEM-orized. "Hi!" I say to the gal. "I'll take a large, iced hazelnut latte, with 2 percent milk, thanks!" The barista wordlessly takes my money and closes the window. Really? So much for customer service. *No tip for that bitch.* I can't believe this is your favorite place.

I take a sip of your drink and, as the pure sugar and espresso course through me, I get it. It tastes like . . . A melted toffee bar. De-fucking-licious.

Next stop? Your husband's golf course! I'm going to learn how to golf today. And you know what they say, being a teacher and all, the best way to learn is to do: practice, practice practice! Time to visit the pro shop and get signed up for lessons.

I walk into the pro shop and take it all in. The ding-dong of the door alarm (noted, no sneaking up on him here!) and the crisp smell of bamboo and rainfall. Like you, it looks like Mr. Cook also has great taste.

"Hello! I'm here because, well, I need golf lessons and I heard you're the guy!" I got myself extra pretty today. I smile big at him. He's looking at me funny. *Dammit. I probably have some of my smoothie in my teeth.* Why do you put so much seedy shit in those? No wonder you two never kiss anymore. I think this will be the last day I have your gross breakfast smoothie.

He laughed. "Yeah, that's me! I'm Pete, the golf pro!"

"Oh, I know!" I exclaimed, before covering for my slip by taking a giant gulp of my latte.

"Ahh, iced latte, I see?" Pete comments. "Hazelnut by chance? My wife is a total addict." He rolls his eyes. "Looks like you guys even go to the same coffee place!"

Ha. Rolling his eyes at his wife???? I knew things weren't so good at home.

"Haha, oh my gosh," I flirt. "It totally is hazelnut! I can't believe you guessed. I think this is meant to be, Mr. Golf Pro!"

Oops. Too far. Too much. Too stalker. I just can't help myself. I try to cover my awkwardness by throwing down a mountain of cash for golf lessons that I can't afford, set to start tomorrow. Mr. Cook must have cleared his calendar, just for me. *Probably wants to get away from you.*

"See you tomorrow . . . I'm sorry. Did I catch your name?" Pete asked.

But before he can get his question out I've done a 180, and I run-walk all the way to my car, making sure my ass bounces the way I know he likes it. I've seen him watch you walk up the same cart path before, Clarissa.

CHAPTER 19:

BUNKERS AND BLUEBERRIES

Jack
Location: Way Far Away, Jack's House
Mood: Proud

JUNE'S THIEVING HABIT BEGAN LONG BEFORE OUR MARRIAGE DID, ALTHOUGH it was unknown to me. Now, you might say it isn't really thieving when it was nonsensical stuff like other people's candy wrappers, but the way I look at it is, keep your mitts off what isn't yours. Really! Is that so hard to grip these days?

So June and I always had a garden when we were married, but when I moved out, I also began growing blueberries at my bachelor pad. Now I'm just kidding because it was more of a *Dad's Den*, but humor got me through my divorce and it will get me through now. That, and my faith, of course.

The first summer harvest was typical, not many berries to speak of. Blueberries are at their prime around the Fourth of July in these parts—bursting with sweet, juicy, purple guts and begging to be eaten straight off the bush. If I could collect enough to fill a small bowl, I'd pour ice-cold milk on them with a spoonful of sugar, just like my mom used to make me for a special treat.

The second harvest was even better, because, first, it was the second harvest, but also, unbeknownst to anyone, I had reburied my blueberry bushes, deeper, which is one of the reasons us Northerners struggle to get a lot of berries at harvest time. Farming, or any sort of growing, is very difficult here. Our winters are nearly nine months long. Very cold. We need to plant our bushes deeper. So I went out one night, under the moonlight, just me, my Marlboros, and my shovel, and I dug five four-foot-deep holes for my blueberry bushes, and replanted them before dawn. Didn't even leave any disrupted dirt. Why in the middle of the night? Looky-loos! People around here are always copying me, from my ham-smoking methods to now, probably, my blueberry-planting methods. Best to keep blueberry-planting secrets under the cover of the dark night sky. That's also where I keep my wild rice secrets.

The third harvest was explosive. Now I mean, explosive. More-fireworks-than-I-buy-in-Indiana-every-year explosive. Berries were bursting off the branches, straight into my bowl. I was delighted. It was about that time that I started dating Ellen, and I think part of my appeal to her was my blueberry skills. Ellen did love her blueberries. And wild rice.

So one night, Ellen and I went out to the movie theater. We come back, and I notice that some of my blueberries are missing. Clearly missing. I get a little obsessive about my blueberries, so I took a photo of them before we left. I snap some more pictures upon arriving home, before touching anything, and compare the pictures. There it is. A whole branch, emptied.

This couldn't be the work of an animal. Not the way that branch was cleared. I deal with rabbits, squirrels, deer, and black bears in my yard every day

I looked around, and saw the unthinkable: All of those stolen blueberries were smashed! Right on my walkway. Now, do you know how hard that is to clean up? And do you know what a waste of good blueberries that is? I was bound and determined to put a stop to the blueberry thief. And I knew exactly whose calling card this was: June!

So a few harvests go by, and this game of stealing and popping perfectly good blueberries continues. I even caught her on my trail camera a few times. Put it right up next to my birdhouse where I knew she wouldn't see it.

Hilarious. She's the worst thief I have ever seen and she ought to not wear her bathrobe when committing crimes, not to mention sins. Very unflattering, and a dead giveaway for me, as June was known to wear her bathrobe out at night.

Then, June meets Sheep, and they move out to *The Way Middle of Nowhere*. I'm tickled because, first, I won't run into her when I'm picking out my porketta at the grocery store, and, at long last, my blueberries will be left alone. So, you can imagine my shock when the blueberry thieving continues. I know June isn't driving back to my house, an hour each way, to rob me of my blueberries. I don't think so, anyway. I decided to ask the neighbor kids, because they're the real watch dogs around here, to see what they know.

And I'll be damned. The neighborhood kids knew everything! Told me right off that June had paid them to keep smashing my blueberries for her. Told them to smash the best, plumpest berries, a few days a week, and not in a distinguishable pattern. Honest to God, that's what she told them kids. So, like any good businessman, I thought on my feet and offered those kids double to officially rat June out, by writing down their side of the story. They didn't need to include their names of course, and I don't know what I'm going to do with it, but this here is theft, and also a broken commandment, and I am the victim. Now that is documented, and will be in my *June* file.

At that point, I knew neighborhood kids and trail cameras weren't going to cut it as a blueberry security team anymore. So, like my father before me, I grabbed my shovel, and decided to make my basement bigger. History repeats itself, you see. My father dug a basement because his family got too big, and I'm digging a bigger basement because of a blueberry thief.

I know my dad is here with me, even though he's passed on. I know because right when I dig the final scoop, Ellen yells at me, "Jack, I'm done with our puzzle! The last piece, it clicked right in!" and that's our thing, me and Dad. Puzzle pieces. Dad definitely helped guide me while building this bunker. And if anyone knew how to dig a bunker, it was my dad, who had lived through real, actual war.

I dug out a gigantic bunker in one weekend, with the secret entrance behind my fake fireplace in the basement family room, which was directly below my precious blueberries. Now, let's not talk about permits here, because the dumbest thing you can do for a secret bunker is get a public permit, but that's not the point.

Next, I worked with someone I had met over the years in the meat trade who had a connection at some fancy technical school, and they helped me create the laser beams that now surround and protect my plants. They are invisible to the naked eye, but they are there, streaming live, twenty-four hours a day, directly to my phone. The phone no one thinks I know how to work. I got the idea from Clarissa's embryos back when she did that fertility stuff. They grew those little um ... well, babies, I guess ... in a tiny incubator where Clarissa could check on them anytime. *Well, that would work perfectly for my blueberries.* And, the rest is history.

Not many people have seen my bunker. Ellen, of course, I trust her with my life. I mean, she got me to quit smoking! And not even from making me or saying anything, just from the look on her face. So yeah, I trust her. I've been smoking since I was seven. *Or was it six?* Anyway, I haven't smoked a cigarette since we got married. Clarissa could take a tip or two, or maybe just hang around Ellen longer and get The Look.

Clarissa has been in the bunker, because she gave me lots of ideas what with the shows she watches, and Pete. That's where I interrogated him when he asked for my daughter's hand in marriage.

Now, my daughter Clarissa has lots of problems, but one is, she doesn't know how to do anything small. So when we designed the bunker, she decided that I had to have exits, other than going back through the fireplace. She thought that was crazy, and there should be multiple exits. I'm glad I listened to her on this one, because she's right. She's a schoolteacher and I know she thinks every day about school shootings, and multiple exits is something she's always blabbing about. Now, I have two exits, which I can't tell you where, but anyway, I have two alternative exits, and at both exits, I have my escape necessities. Clarissa designed all this too, and again, it's perfect.

Both exits have a single cupboard, from floor to ceiling, which isn't super high, because this is more of a crawl space, and a lockbox. In the cupboard are my costume options. So far, she has curated a Butcher on His Lunch Break costume, an Elderly Grandpa with a Cane costume (the cane is cleverly hollow and includes things I can't tell you, but my medications are one!), a Gardener costume, a Construction Worker costume, and just for fun, a Luigi costume. Her sense of humor, that one! And of course, my electric scooter. I've gotten that baby up to twenty-five miles per hour now, although Ellen thinks it's twelve miles per hour. Don't want to scare her! The scooter is always charging and I have a few scooters, so I don't mind keeping a couple at my exits. With gas prices and all, I made sure to find some good electric scooters for cheap until we get a new president.

In the fireproof lockbox are a few more escape necessities. Passports, glue-on mustaches, instant hair dye, a ball cap for a meat brand I hate, and a sock. In that sock is the most important thing. My petty cash. I always tell Clarissa you need to have some petty cash. Some walking-around-money. Just in case this county goes to shit, have some cash. And boy do I. I keep my cash in socks all over the place. I don't mind telling you about this one sock because it's one of several and my bunker is impenetrable.

So, I have a bunker, and I have blueberries. And now you know why.

CHAPTER 20:

CLEAN THAT MOUTH UP

Clarissa

Location: My Comfy Bed

Mood: Shocked

"HEY BABYCAKES, BIG NEWS!" MY DAD YELL-TALKS.

"Dad? It's 5:00 a.m. You better have bigger fucking news than the FBI showing up on your doorstep, so be my guest."

My dad laughs. "Even better! We're coming to visit!"

Silence.

"When?"

Silencer.

"Dad. When." I rip off my cold gel eyemask and, while my eyes are being pierced with bright light, I dig around in my mouth, trying to pull out my retainer like a disoriented chicken.

"Today. Um . . . actually . . ."

"Actually what, Dad?"

"Um . . . we're just about packed up and ready to go."

"What the fuck Dad!!!!" I yell.

"Clarissa Lee Macellaio! I'm counting now and that is your second 'fuck' in thirty seconds. You know I do not condone that language, nor does Ellen, nor does the Lord. Well, I'm okay with it if I say it from time to time, but not my daughter, oh no. I don't care if you grew up in a butcher shop and I don't care how old you think you are, little missy. You can clean that mouth up by the time we get there, okay? And honey? We can't wait to see you!"

"Now," he continued, "Don't be worrying about us, honey. I know how you are (Read: neurotic). We'll get a motel, either the Bates or the Norman where we have stayed before, I think, and we are A-okay to take care of ourselves. Now. Do you know which one has a better continental breakfast? None of those weird, hard-boiled eggs in a liquid packet and a nutrigrain bar or anything, one with a real, spinning waffle iron and maybe, I don't know, a nice oatmeal spread for Ellen?"

And with that my dad clicked his happy ass right off the phone and my day was totally and completely ruined.

I get off the call after promising to send him the phone number for the hotel.

"Yes, Dad, it will go straight to the hotel, I promise. No, Dad, it won't go to a call center in China. Yes, Dad, I know how you feel about call centers in China. Yes, Dad, I'm well aware that your grandparents immigrated here from Italy and picked up the language real quick."

For the record I am way too fucking tired, oops sorry, to provide you stats on the number of languages spoken in the USA, but I want to remind you that, by most estimates, there are around 450 different languages spoken in this beautiful melting pot. Now that is a beautiful thing!

"Yes, Dad, I know you prayed in school." (Psst, so did I, you sent me to Catholic school for ten long years, remember? I do. And so do my teachers. They didn't like all the stories I wrote, especially the one impressively named 'The Fire' that I wrote in fourth grade. They wanted a drama, and that's what I gave them. A drama. Basically, a fire burned down the whole family's house and some of them died. Listen. That's horrible and tragic and awful, I know.

But, they wanted drama, and dramas should be realistic, and realistically, fire is going to win, most of the time, at least. So, anyway, I'm sorry it seems prayer in school didn't seem to help me much, Dad).

I love my dad, I really do. But it's way too fucking early for this. My day was clearly ruined, so I put my earbuds in, press play on *Signs of a Psychopath*, and go back to sleep.

CHAPTER 21:

iNTO THE RAT CAGE

Marge
Location: Leroy's Dirty Room
Mood: Gloomy

I look around at the giant mess I've made in Leroy's room. He's gone extra long today, working a double on the road for some rat infestation in a different county, so I have plenty of time.

I'm not sure what exactly I'm looking for, but there must be at least the life insurance paperwork in this shithole, somewhere. I can't do much about it now without Leroy finding out, but I can at least burn the paperwork and make it harder for him when I croak.

Is this what my life has come to? Sure, I wasn't a nun or anything, but I tried the best with what I had and, for whatever reason, the Lord dealt me a shit hand from the very beginning, starting with my rotten parents. Dead for the better part of two decades, they weren't worth thinking about.

No, I think, it was that rotten husband of mine and his vile offspring that really did me in. I am convinced someone must have swapped my precious babies with evil little monsters at the hospital when they were born. From the very beginning, they were awful. Born just thirteen months apart, they shared a special connection. My little Irish twins, I liked to call them, in the rare moments that I felt we might be bonding.

I am just about done putting everything back in its place, so I can still catch *Jeopardy*, because I don't miss the old Alex reruns, never a day, not one. I feel the urge to vomit as the different smells from Leroy's room permeate my nasal passages. You know, the ones that won't ever leave? Food and sweat and rat shit covering everything, including his DVD collection, *The 40 Year Old Virgin* at the very top.

As I look up at the rat cage in the corner of the room, I notice something. Something shiny at the bottom of the cage, buried in rat droppings and newspaper scraps. I move closer to the tank. It's so dirty it's hard to tell for sure. Could be one of his little rat babies, Lord knows how many are in there these days. And the creepy sicko feeds them frog babies. Tiny little things.

As I get closer, I notice that the object is about the size of my hand and very shiny. I can't help myself. I close my eyes, reach in, and pull out the object. It's heavier than it looks, and in the few seconds it takes for me to unjam it, I can feel wet little rat snouts tickling my hand with their wiry whiskers.

I finally get it out and shake my hand, like that will get the rat germs off or something. I hold the object in my palm, up to the light. It's glittering and shining in the light. It was so beautiful! What on earth was this doing in the rat cage? I don't recognize it. At least it isn't mine. I figure Leroy stole it from someone, although I can't take a stab at who, because people who have a pretty jewelry box like this would have absolutely nothing to do with my son.

I pull at the top, wiggling it a little bit, as there is some old congealed rat piss on it, making the edges stick together. Leroy. He ruins everything he has. Mucks it right up, he does. I pull a little harder, and the top pops open. And in it, I find five tiny items. A jade oval earring, a delicate anklet with little crystals dangling from it, a silver house key, a ruby-studded cross necklace, and a tooth.

CHAPTER 22:

THE ODD COLLECTOR

Leroy
Location: On the phone
Mood: Terrified

"MOM'S GOTTA GO." I WAS OUT OF BREATH WHEN MOLLY FINALLY ANSWERED.

"Go? Like where? To the senior center? Or back from the hell she crawled out of?" Molly cackles.

"Number two," I whisper. "I mean option two. Not like bathroom two. Sorry, confusing."

I can almost see Molly rolling her eyes at me. I am always saying something stupid at the wrong time. Thankfully, she lets it slide.

"Ohhhhh. I see. You really wanna kill Mom? Now? We aren't even close to the life insurance policy maturing. If she croaks now, we're looking at basically nothing, plus funeral costs. Think about that, you dummy."

"Well, if we wait, we might both be spending the rest of our life in fucking prison you dumb bitch!" I explode.

"Wait, back up? What are you—"

"She found it! She found my box! Molly! The box. Mom has it!" I whimper.

"Oh, Leroy. I told you to stop doing that. You weird fucker. What is wrong with you? No wonder you can't find a girlfriend." Molly just loves chastising me. Just because she's thirteen months older than me means absolutely nothing. Plus, she is technically a woman, even though I don't really think about her like that, because she's my sister, but, yeah, women's opinions are meaningless and worthless.

"Shut up, you bitch!" I scream.

"No. Leroy, I'm goddamn serious. I told you to stop keeping those girls' things a long time ago. It's weird."

"Oh, shut up! Just shut up! There's a lot weirder shit going on around here than some jewelry in a box."

"And a tooth! Did you forget about the tooth, you psycho!" Molly rages. "Mom could have figured it out by now! Dammit Leroy. All of those items were shared on the news at some point. She's going to recognize it! And then, when the cops come sniffing around here and see that all the women around you are missing teeth . . . I mean, come the fuck on Leroy!"

I groan. "This is why I fucking called you, Molly, clean your ears out. Like I said, Mom's got to go."

CHAPTER 23:

DRY MOUTH

Clarissa
Location: The Little Gray House
Mood: Paranoid

I THINK I'M GOING CRAZY. EITHER THAT, OR I'M BEING STALKED. THE MOST likely answer, honestly, is that the medical cannabis gummies I've been taking for the last few days have been extra strong. And I mean extra strong. The kind of gummy that might have you laying on your bed staring at the ceiling for eight days, kind of strong. My doctor told me to eat a scoop of peanut butter on an empty stomach prior to devouring my medical treats. She explained that it would make me twice as high for half the price. She used more fancy, medical terms, but that's the summary. My kind of girl.

But really, I must be losing my mind. Everything is just wrong. It's not really explainable, without sounding like a whack job, but I know my house. And I know when something is off. Call it mother's instinct or an unhealthy true crime addiction, but I know that something is going on and I'm going to figure out exactly what.

Just right after I have a big snack, take a nap, and drink a gallon of water. Now that sounds nice. And as so often happens to us busy moms, by the time I woke up I forgot about my feeling of unease, my intuition that something was just not right.

CHAPTER 24:

i SCARED YOU

Molly

Location: Molly's Creepy Brain

Mood: Haunting

A LITTLE FRIDGE REARRANGING.

A book moved to a different shelf.

A picture of you and your bestie: gone.

Burned up, actually. It was a horrible picture of you, anyway.

A pair of your leggings gone: They will look great on me.

A tee shirt of your husband's that you love, tucked under my pillow so I can smell what you smell.

Your diary. Oh god. I wanted to take it so badly, but I couldn't find it. I wanted to read your innermost thoughts and desires. Everything you can't say out loud, I know you probably wrote down. I saw you lots of times, digging through your purse for something to write with. Something to write on. Sometimes your diary, sometimes a scrap of paper.

The other day, you dropped the scrap of paper you had scribbled on. I wanted to chase you down, to give it back, to interact with you, but I wanted that paper with your private thoughts more.

I opened up the paper as soon as you were far enough away. On it, just a few words.

"Dear Diary, Today I met a potential best friend at the school assembly. She seems so cool. I hope she wants to be my friend, too! Writing this down so I don't forget our meet-a-versary in case this works out! Eek!"

My heart skips a million beats. Those words! They were about me! I knew you felt the same way about me. I just knew it! I calm down a little bit, knowing I'm not under so much pressure. I can relax a little bit. You like me!

CHAPTER 25:

CHICAGO FAMS AND MAFIA HAMS

Jack

Location: Way Far Away

Mood: Excited!

"Well, here we go El! I've got the car packed and the map routed!" I yell. I never did trust that GPS garbage anyway. What's wrong with a good old map? You know what that is, don't you? Government tracking.

I'm rambling, I know. But hell, I'm nervous. I'm skipping town on the FBI! Ha! Me! Can you believe it? I just don't like how they're badgering me about my political views. I did nothing wrong and, as I have mentioned numerous times, I have never in my life been east of Chicago. I mean, are they banging on the Democrat's doors, interrupting family dinner? I don't think so. It's another way this country has been ruined. I'm not letting anyone scare me, not even the FBI.

Like I told them. I am a Patriot, a Trump supporter, and a gun owner.

They got nothing . . . because there is nothing!

But now . . . now they're dragging my cousin and his family into this. The entire Macellaio family, probably. Our reputations tarnished! My cousin and his family, by the way, live in Chicago and I haven't spoken to them since the nineties. Back when I used to deliver hams to the area every Christmas. Yep. Big order to the Chicago community back then. Fine people of Chicago really appreciated my secret ham-smoking method. Turns out the FBI doesn't believe me and finds this suspicious. I can't believe they had a photograph of my van. I wonder if I can get a copy? Always did like that model.

I'm Italian. We're immigrants. I can't help it that part of my family is in the Mafia! And it certainly doesn't mean that I am. Nor does it mean I was at the Capitol on January 6.

CHAPTER 26:

CATHOLIC GUILT AND SHAME

Clarissa

Location: The Little Gray House

Mood: Frantic

HIDE THE WEED, HIDE THE ALCOHOL, HIDE THE SEX TOYS, AND HIDE THE nudey tapes! Take out the crosses and the Bible we got from Dad for our wedding! Don't forget that ugly candlestick Mom got us for the wedding. It was a gift from both my mom and dad, my mom insisted, my dad probably paid for it. It's ugly and it lives in my laundry room. It's 9:00 a.m., and I'm exhausted by this little family reunion already. No ugly candlestick today, I decide.

I love it when my dad comes to visit, but I get a little crazy. I am old enough that I shouldn't care, but I will always care what my dad thinks, because he's my dad and he raised me right. At least I'm not on birth control anymore, don't have to worry about him finding those again.

I try to think of what current secrets I have from my dad so I know what he will be nosing around for while he's here. I have one more tattoo— or is it two?—since I saw him last. Most of my tattoos I've hidden for more than a decade before he has seen them. Unfortunately, in order to do that, you have to get them in pretty provocative places. No new piercings, no illegitimate children, no big CD orders billed to him from Columbia Records I'm worried about him finding. I actually have the job he thinks I have, which hasn't always been true. What? I don't want to disappoint my dad, ever. This should be a pretty easy visit, not many secrets between us these days! I love it like that!

I'm sure they will be here shortly. I can't get over what may have inspired this last-minute trip. I talk to my dad all the time, every morning before he goes for coffee, at 5:30 a.m. He doesn't just pop up like this. I have some ideas, but my dad's a hard guy to pin down. He likes it that way.

At least I'll get to hear the whole FBI experience in person. I'm still a little jealous about the whole thing. I need to know all the details.

CHAPTER 27:

TWO LiTTLE MONSTERS

Marge
Location: Leroy's Bedroom
Mood: Afraid

I SHOULD HAVE KNOWN, I SAY OVER AND OVER IN MY HEAD. I MEAN, I KNOW I bred two little monsters, but this is a stretch even for our family.

I take the little silver box out of the extra-large Preparation-H jar I've been storing it in. I cleaned it, don't worry. But I don't want Leroy to know I have it, and if there is one thing that I can keep private around here it is my hemorrhoid cream. Not much else, believe me.

I hold them all in my hand and close my eyes. But not the tooth. I am so afraid of that tooth. It's beautiful—pearly and white, dainty. It looks like a woman's tooth. Wait. Do men and women have different-looking teeth? I'm not sure, but I don't like it, not one bit. I might be old, but I ain't senile. . . I think. I know what I'm looking at. And I remember. I saw it on my news program. I know people think I'm senile, just because I never leave this house, and I'm eighty-five, but I'm sharp as a tack. I don't even need to search it up, like the young people these days. Do they even know anything anymore?

These murders happened pretty much in my own backyard. It started two years ago, about this same time of year, early to mid-summer.

The first victim was a beautiful nurse. She worked night shifts at the local hospital and, after an odd run in with a woman at the emergency unit where she worked, she disappeared. Never seen again. When her body was found and the poor girl's family had to identify it, they noticed right away that something was wrong. They had seen her leave for work that evening, and her coworkers corroborated it. The pretty nurse, Gloria, was missing the ruby cross necklace her grandfather had given her just that very same afternoon. The hospital was never able to figure out who the woman that visited was. She was named as a suspect, but they kept hitting dead ends. Eventually, the case went cold and her poor family had no daughter and no one to blame.

Then, later that summer, right after the Fourth of July in fact, there was another one. This time, the victim was a lawyer. She worked for a divorce firm in town and was known by everyone to be the best. She was especially good at taking men for everything they had, and the men around here knew it. I think the story went that her sister had identified her body, the poor thing. She noticed that Lily was missing a dainty gold anklet, with little crystals dangling from it. She wore it every day. With everything. Plus, the selfie she had posted the day she went missing showed her wearing it. They knew a man had come to visit Lily about a contentious divorce. He insisted on meeting her outside of the office, and she did, because Lily really tried to do best for her clients. She had the appointment written in her planner, one of the cute ones, with the stickers and such. She was never seen again. And same as last time, a bunch of dead ends with the guy, but they suspect he had something to do with it.

The third girl was never found. Her name was Rachel and she was a runner. She ran every morning at 5:00 a.m., like clockwork. One day, she never came back from her run. Her ring was found near the bike path in a small, wooded area. They didn't come up with many clues in Julia's case. Her family identified the ring and was pretty sure she had it on the day she went missing, as it was her engagement ring and she was very superstitious and had not removed it once since becoming engaged two years earlier. They also found some blood by the trees as well. Not much, but more than a papercut and less than a murder scene, but it did match her blood type and I think they did eventually confirm that it matched her DNA.

Number four was a community worker of some sort. I remember being so sad about that, someone who helps people for a living. And underpaid, considering. She was such a good person. I'm sure it's hard being in the social-type services, and I feel like families are going to probably hate you either way, whether you do the right thing and remove a kid when needed or do the wrong thing and leave a kid in a home, or vice versa. None of it is black and white. I couldn't do it, and I commend anyone who does.

I remember the social worker we had in our life when my kids were young. I had to lie to her. I had no choice, or my husband would have killed me. But my kids liked her and I think they secretly hoped she would whisk them away, far away, and plop them in a house, any house, where they felt safe and didn't have to view violence every day, and be a victim to it. That changed when the social worker closed our case. Leroy was so angry. He, especially, had really liked Jolinda, the social worker. Once she closed the case, when Leroy was eight and Molly was nine, he refused to talk about her. He refused to say her name. And he especially refused to have anything to do with social services, ever again. I can hardly blame him. Anyway, they found this missing social worker, missing an earring, in the alley behind one of her clients houses. Again, no cameras, no witnesses, but the client she was meeting turned out to be nonexistent, so they thought that was the murderer, but no one actually lived at the address where they found her. It was a daily rental with an untraceable renter. I have a friend who recently told me about a show I can watch on some streaming thing and it sounds so similar to the life I lived with my children.

Then, around fall sometime, I think it may have actually been Halloween night now that I think of it. Yes. It was. Anyway, a fifth girl goes missing.. They found her body the next day, before the sun came up. Figure they missed the killer by minutes. By then, the cops were getting frustrated and they called in the FBI. The FBI comes in, which makes the city cops madder once they start dealing with them and see how they kind of like to take over, and we don't really ever get an update after that. Amber was a waitress, and she was one of the best I've personally been served by. I'm sad about all the murdered girls, but I'm most sad about Amber. Probably because I knew her for a long time. I remember thinking she was so funny. She always wore the same bright red color on her nails, and I asked her what it was, and I could never believe what that quippy girl told me. She said, "It's called, I'm Not a Waitress."

Now Amber, she was a little bit different. In her case, the cops had it narrowed down to a strange couple who ate at the diner. Now, they didn't have surveillance cameras or anything, as we don't usually need them around here. Well, I guess we do because look at all the dead girls. Anyway, Frank, over at the diner, he didn't have them and everyone knew it. The cops figure that this couple might be the man and woman from the first two cases. Back to how Amber was different. She wasn't missing anything. Well, let me correct myself. She wasn't missing any jewelry. She was missing a tooth. Right in the front. On Halloween, nonetheless. What a sicko.

So that leaves me with this house key. I don't recognize it. Maybe there is another dead girl I don't know about. Or . . . maybe Leroy has his eye on someone new.

I curse my rotten children under their breath. I had wondered when I saw all those girls turn up basically in a circle around our house, but I wasn't sure and I didn't want to see it.

CHAPTER 28:

i'M READY FOR YOU

Molly
Location: Molly's Bed with Dirty Sheets
Mood: Orgasmic

EVERYTHING IS SO PERFECT. I FEEL LIKE I KNOW EVERYTHING THERE IS TO know about you. I've been wearing your clothes and your perfume, sleeping in your husband's shirt, rolling it around on all my best parts. He really does smell delicious. I've dubbed it, *Sexy Dad*. Sometimes when I'm wearing his shirt and I get a whiff of your perfume I'm wearing, I almost feel like I am you, you know? They say scents are one of the most powerful connections there are to our emotions. I believe it. I'm intoxicated by both of your smells blending together, and I fall asleep with my hands down my panties, thinking about both of you.

CHAPTER 29:

LiTTLE MiSS PRiSS

Leroy
Location: Leroy's Nasty Thoughts
Mood: Shitty

SOMETIMES YOU GOTTA DO SHITTY THINGS. IT'S JUST PART OF LIFE. AT least that's how I think of things. Everything is a tradeoff. Can't have a little fun without a little work, right?

Some people's shitty is shittier than others. Like that bitch in the gray house. I bet that little priss has never had to contemplate murder on a Tuesday afternoon.

I think about her tits again, so perfect under her nightgown. My dick literally groans, stands up and, as quickly as it had arrived it disappeared, flopping over like one of those wacky, waving tube guys on top of the car dealership.

Fucking bitch.

CHAPTER 30:

DON'T FORGET THE CHOCOLATES

Jack

Location: Hotel Norman in the Big City
Mood: Relieved

"Knock, Knock". I hear a loud bang on our motel door. The one to the outside.

"El, can you get that? I'm on the stool!" I yell. "Tell 'em we don't need any more towels, but we do need more of those free chocolates they left on my pillow!"

Silence.

"El! The chocolates!"

Nothing.

Cripes almighty. Do I have to do everything around here? I barely get my ass wiped and my pants pulled up, setting my Archie comic down for later. Hopefully I'll be reading that with some fresh chocolates if El can get her shit together and get me some. I'm sorry. I love her. I really do. Best thing that's ever happened to me, actually. I'm just hungry and I'm nervous about this whole FBI thing.

I walk out of the shitter and run damn near into none other than Rat-Face and Baldy.

"Mr. Macellaio? I thought we advised you to stay in town?" squeaked Rat-Face.

"Well, surely I can complete my visit to see my daughter? This is America, right? Or have I warped to China overnight?" I chuckle.

They aren't laughing.

Baldy clears his throat. "Mr. Macellaio. This is a serious matter. We would appreciate your cooperation."

"I am cooperating!" I yelled.

"Well. Ahem. Um," Rat-Face stuttered. "While we work on confirming your alibi, we need you to stay put."

"And stay put I will, Rat-Face! I mean. Shit. What's your name?"

Rat-Face and Baldy glare at me. "We expect you to finish up this little family trip in the next forty-eight hours and return to your county of residence. Now Mr. Macellaio? That's an order, not a suggestion."

I salute them in acknowledgement as they walk away.

"Now, El, did you get those chocolates?" I ask.

CHAPTER 31:

DENIM CARPENTER SHORTS

Clarissa
Location: Little Gray House
Mood: Arrogant

I kicked Joseph down to the neighbors so I could get the house picked up before Dad and Ellen arrived. Don't worry, I've background checked them, obviously. Honestly, this is the part I hate about family visits. I just get so stressed and I want everything perfect.

I see an extended-cab black truck drive by. It wouldn't be weird, but it's the fourth time I've seen this truck since last night. What in the world? I take the garbage out so I can take a better look. You spy on me, I'm going to spy right back at ya, you know?

As I walk out the door and turn at the garage, I bump into two oafs in suits. Black, fancy suits with sunglasses. My garbage flies from my hands and hits the ground, nearly breaking open.

"Mrs. Cook, I presume?"

"Depends on who's asking," I reply arrogantly.

"The FBI, ma'am. Would you like to see our badges?"

The goddamn FBI followed my dad all the way to my house, seven hours away? This is going too far. I'm left with no other choice but to invite the FBI in. I hope my stash is hidden, since medical or not, it's still illegal federally. Confusing.

I'm even more embarrassed that my neighbor, Dan, saw all of this. He's standing there, watching it all, I'm sure wondering why two undercover-looking police officers are at my doorstep. I like Dan and all, but he can be nosy. At least he's gotten better dressed since he met his wife. But those denim carpenter shorts have got to go.

CHAPTER 32:

i SEE YOUR HUSBAND

Molly

Location: Molly's Nasty Thoughts

Mood: Lustful

I'M STARTING TO REALLY LOVE THIS SHIRT FROM YOUR HUSBAND. THE SMELL, it's just so intoxicating. It's so soft when I wear it and I like to pretend it's his big arms around me. It's starting to be the perfect blend of Peter and me, our scents swirled around, lusting over each other. Your smell is fading fast. Basically gone.

I started my golf lessons! I'm a little giddy every time I get to see your husband, but can I tell you a secret? I think he enjoys seeing me, too. The way he looks at me is just so . . . I can feel it. I've started bringing him a coffee when I see him, it's our little thing. I know he appreciates me.

Today I'm getting ready to go visit him. Not for our lesson. No, he isn't expecting me today. I actually made him lunch because I know you mentioned he gets so hungry, what with his long hours and all. I know he'll love it, and he'll see how kind, thoughtful, and special I am, too.

CHAPTER 33:

SNOWFLAKES

Jack
Location: The Hotel Room at Hotel Norman
Mood: Triggered

"Ellen, are you ready?" I yell.

"Jack, we're in the same hotel room. you don't have to yell." Ellen is puttering with her yarn. Thankfully we got an extra bed for all of her supplies. She is always knitting something, that one.

"Whoops! Sorry about that! I'm just excited is all. Let's get going over to Clarissa's before those two goons come back."

I was in such a happy mood to see my daughter and escape Rat-Face and Baldy that I almost missed seeing the other vehicle parked outside my daughter's house.

None other than one black extended-cab truck. At least my ex-wife isn't here, with her motorcycle, the one with the side-car. Only thing that could make this worse, in fact.

I haven't seen my ex-wife since . . . was it Pete and Clarissa's wedding? No. The going away party. The one to send them off to the commune. Clarissa reassured me it wasn't a nudist colony or anything—can you imagine? I mean, I happen to know my ex-wife also enjoys going to country music festivals where it's known full well that the women flash their, um . . . their, you know . . .

Anyway, there Ellen and I were, out to the local Strawberry Goose Cafe for dinner and walked into this whole party. I'm talking a party. Now, this isn't a place where parties are really common, or preferred, really. It's more of a place you go to after church, or for a nice quiet dinner with your bride on Friday—if you're a real Catholic and fast from meat every Friday like I do—for a walleye sandwich and coleslaw and strong coffee.

So, our sandwiches were just being delivered and about thirty people walk into the cafe. Now this place isn't big, you know. Just a little local restaurant in a small town. And they have decorations in their hands. Bags of them. Just about my worst nightmare.

Probably going to be a bunch of yelling kids running around, I thought, and I hate that. Can't people keep their kids quiet at restaurants anymore? I'm no fuddy-duddy, just ask my grandson Joseph. I mean Corndog. Hey, I'm trying. Even he understands that restaurants are a situation where children should definitely be seen, not heard.

So, the party walks in and, before I can gather my thoughts, my ex-wife June pops right out of the middle of the crowd and plops down, right at my table! I can't make this shit up. So, she sits down, and I'm sitting there, just trying to eat my fish and not eat red meat, which is hard enough when you're a butcher by name and a meat-cutter by trade. So there I was, craving a big, fat juicy steak, and instead, I have my ex-wife breathing on my coleslaw.

"Well, Jack," she says, "you are going to be thrilled to hear."

And she waits. So I wait.

I know this trick. She wants me to ask.

So I'm not going to. Don't have to.

"Well, aren't you going to ask?" she says coyly, batting her eyelashes. Ellen kicks me under the table and rolls her eyes. I roll mine right along with

her. *Best thing to do, when you're in this type of situation. Side with the current wife. Always. Pretty simple. Don't understand how men get so wrapped up in bickering.*

"Nope."

"Jack!" she says, exasperated. "You're so rude! Well, anyway. If you're not going to ask, I'm going to tell you. Because you are not going to ruin my night. As you can see, there is a party here at the Strawberry Goose, and it's for me and Sheep, not you." She looks at Ellen. "Ellen, I'm so sorry. This is between me and Jack. Did you want to step out to the ladies room, maybe freshen up or something?"

"Nope," Ellen says, narrowing her eyes and clutching the Miraculous Medal around her neck.

Oh boy, I think. This is getting good. When Ellen brings the medal out, I know it's about to go down. I might be getting old, but two ladies bickering over you? Never gets old, I tell ya.

"Ellen isn't leaving and I don't really give two shits, so spit it out or don't, sweetheart," I say. *Ha! That's a good one. Notebook material, for sure.*

"Fine," June relents, tossing her hair over her shoulder. *She's grown it out long these days, so long it's about down to her buttocks and an interesting gray color, sort of like a mop. Maybe they don't believe in scissors over at the commune.*

The rest of the night was uneventful, as June enjoyed her party and Ellen and I scarfed down our fish sandwiches so that we could get out of there. My daughter Clarissa had just gotten me set up with Hulu and given me a whole list of interesting shows to watch. We always did enjoy our TV together. Ellen may be hesitant. The last program Clarissa recommended was called Beef and it was not about a butcher or meat and had lots of swearing and nudity in it. I thought it was great, but when I stopped watching it Ellen stopped gripping her medal so much, so . . . Maybe I would stick with Back to the Future, I decide, as we drove back to our house and left June's Strawberry Soiree a distant memory.

Now, you might wonder why I didn't just keep driving my merry ass right back to the hotel. Well. I don't run away from my problems. That's part of what's wrong with kids today: snowflakes, the whole lot of them.

So, I stand up extra tall, tuck my bride into my side, and ring Clarissa's doorbell.

CHAPTER 34:

THE CiRCUS

Leroy
Location: The Little Gray House
Mood: Anticipatory

I pull up to the little gray house on the hill. It's busier than normal. I see two cars I haven't seen here before. I make a mental note to ask Molly.

Aside from her Jeep, there's an extended-cab black truck, illegal tint if I may mention . . . interesting. A burgundy Honda is on the street, half blocking the driveway. Does she have the fucking circus here? The truck is parked right in the middle of the driveway. I hate people that take up two parking spots with one car.

I wonder if I should come back later, but I want to see her, and I know her Ring cam has already captured my face. It would be weirder and more suspicious to turn back now.

Who am I kidding? I don't give two shits if my own mother is here. I bet she would like those perfect little tits, too. I ring the doorbell, and finally get an answer after what feels like ages. The only good thing, or pitiful thing, I suppose, when you consider how infrequent it is, is that my hard-on is gone.

It's kind of more like a deflated balloon, and although I'm sad to see it go, I know how to get it back.

You open the door and your mouth is half open, like you were in the middle of saying something. I see your pretty little teeth. Gosh, have I noticed them before? I feel my crotch start to tingle.

"Yes?" You're clearly annoyed. This was a quicker job than most. We have lots going on at a time. Usually we have more time to make people feel comfortable after stalking them for a few months, figuring them out. Comfortable or not, this bitch would have her face in my lap by tomorrow and there wasn't a damn thing she could do about it.

"I've come to collect my trap. Unless you've noticed any mice signs? Shit? Anything like that?"

Her face says she's listening, but I can tell she isn't. She doesn't want to let me in. I can tell. But there's company here and she isn't alone, so she feels safe. I can almost see her think.

And she opens the door, and she lets me in.

CHAPTER 35:

NO COFFEE FOR YOU

Clarissa

Location: Little Gray House
Mood: Chaotic

THIS IS AN ABSOLUTE SHIT SHOW, I TOOK AROUND MY LIVING ROOM AGAIN. So much for a peaceful fucking morning. Plus, I have some creep running around my basement and I can't even check on him every three minutes as I would prefer. I haven't seen him since he arrived.

It all started with running into the FBI in my driveway. Now, normally this would make me super excited and I'd probably fangirl them, make them coffee, and try to get some good stories out of them. But, I wasn't in the mood today. And besides, they are here about a case of mistaken identity. It isn't even interesting. Literally something a town cop could handle, but no, let's bring in the whole FBI.

My dad was next to arrive, and I've never been more relieved to see him! I gave him and Ellen a huge hug before they had to deal with those two lugs. No coffee with the FBI today, I thought to myself. Dang it.

No sooner could I pour myself, Dad, and Ellen a beautiful, hand-crafted cup of piping-hot coffee than my doorbell rang again. I'm seething inside. It's 2023. Text first if it's an emergency and you need to just show up, or how about, you just don't show up to people's houses like that. Ever.

I open the door, and I swear if I hadn't been so diligent about doing my Kegels after I had Joseph, I would have pissed myself right then and there. But, I smiled, clenched my pelvic floor, and said, "Mom! Come in!" I really should get Botox. At least then I would be able to hide my surprise, or rather, shock.

Like my dad, my mom didn't visit often. And when she does visit, it's for Joseph's birthday. No more, no less. His birthday is more than nine months away at this point, so I'm not sure what I owe this pleasure to. You see, my mom and I don't have a lot in common anymore. Not since she moved off the grid, anyway. I'm not even sure she likes me too much these days. We got into quite the tiff about this commune move and things haven't been the same since.

I step aside, as she and Sheep cross the threshold and take in the scene. I can't help laughing to myself on account of the stark juxtaposition between Sheep's baldness and my mom's insanely long hair, but am rudely interrupted by my mom.

"Helloooooo, Jack!" my mom croons.

CHAPTER 36:

i BROUGHT YOU LUNCH

Molly

Location: Molly's Car
Mood: Perturbed

You weren't there when I brought you lunch. I tried getting more information from the girl at the counter, but she was useless. I left the lunch I made especially for you with her, regretting it instantly.

Doesn't Clarissa worry about all those women you have working for you? They all wear skirts and talk about you like you're so important. I would be worried, but I wouldn't need to be, because I would just work for you and we could go to work together and I could pack both of our lunches and there wouldn't be anyone to worry about.

Is that creepy? I don't really have a good gauge of what other people find creepy. My brother tells me I smother people, like butter on hot corn. He told me to watch some *Window* movie but I'm not sure what he means. I don't understand what the problem is, anyway. Don't people want to be cared about, to be loved, to be seen? Isn't that what we all want?

I get back in my car and head to the cemetery outside of town. I have some people to see.

CHAPTER 37:

A FAMILY REUNION

Jack

Location: Little Gray House

Mood: Sarcastic

THIS SCENE IS LIKE SOMETHING FROM ONE OF MY JOKES. IT STARTS SOMEthing like this: So, a guy walks into a bar, and there are two FBI agents and his ex-wife. Ha! I never was sure what to call Sheep these days. Domestic partner, wasn't it? Crazy, all that language-changing business. Seems like I'm always saying the wrong thing. All these new words these snowflakes have invented recently. It's ridiculous. Probably would never have happened if they kept religion in school. Pretty simple.

Anyway, I'm sitting here, on sensory overload, not really knowing where to look or what to say, so I don't. I just shut up. Between Rat-Face, Baldy, and my ex-wife, I don't feel like talking much. Suddenly I wish I was still a smoker. Maybe I should sneak into Clarissa's medical reefer stash and see what she's always blabbing about. Although I was against it initially, it has helped her manage her PTSD from all that baby-loss business, so maybe it could work in this situation. I'm not against all change you know, just dumb change.

My ex-wife is prattling on to the FBI agents. Of course she is. Probably will invite them over for drinks later. I snicker. Not sure where you can invite them to when you live off the grid . . . your tent? Ridiculous.

Rat-Face, Baldy, and June are staring at me.

I realize I'm laughing out loud on accident instead of in my head. "Uh, sorry," I mutter. I turn on my confidence. "What's going on, fellas! Long time no see! What brings you boys by?"

Rat-Face glares at me. I glare right back. Best way to intimidate a rat.

"We were just leaving, Mr. Macellaio," Baldy says.

"Well, get on then," I say, puffing up my chest. I might be little, but they don't call me Tiger for nothing!

The air is tense. June is standing right next to me, fiddling with her hair. Are those the start of dreadlocks? Or maybe it's just uncombed hair. I attempt to make conversation. "So, June, how's life off the grid going? Enjoying things?"

"Eat shit, Jack," she says, and walks away.

CHAPTER 38:

BAD BREATH

Leroy
Location: Molly's Apartment
Mood: Dark and Foreboding

"Did you do it?" Molly whispers. Her breath stinks.

"Of course I did it. I always do what you tell me," I whisper back. "Jesus! Get a fucking breath mint, would ya?"

Molly recoils, just as I knew she would. That's one way to get that bitch to back down, make her feel like shit about herself, just like our old man used to. I watch as she blows her rancid breath on her hand and sniffs it, wrinkling her nostrils. *Told, ya, you nasty bitch. You stink.*

"Where is she?" Molly asks.

"Why should I tell you?" I hiss angrily. "You always make me do your shit work and it's not fair! I'm so sick of it. And now Mom's dead, and we have to try to hide this until the policy matures, which is in eight fucking months, Molly. Do you get that? So yeah, I'm pissed, and even though Mom's a bitch and probably getting eaten by worms as we speak, I'm not going to tell you where I put her. Because I know it will piss you off".

Molly is seething. I've seen this face before, a few times. Every time I see it, I know someone is about to die.

CHAPTER 39:

THE DRINK THIEF

Clarissa

Location: Little Gray House on the Hill

Mood: Awkward

MY PARENTS ARE IN THE SAME ROOM FOR THE FIRST TIME IN GOD KNOWS how long. I mean, my sisters and I even sat them at separate tables for our weddings to make sure our special days weren't awkward. That's why it was so weird that my mom insisted on giving Pete and I a joint wedding present. That she picked out by herself, I'm sure.

And now, with the stress of this FBI stuff, not to mention me losing my mind, they were seated in my living room and staring at me like puppy dogs. I am almost forty years old, I tell myself. Not my problem. But it is. It always is. Forever the peacemaker with these two, and for what? It doesn't last.

"Well, this is awkward," I say. I reach in the fridge to upgrade my coffee to vodka, because obviously, but to my dismay, my six pack of special spritzers is gone. I hate alcohol, and hardly ever drink. I surely have not drunk those six little gems. I'm salivating at the thought of the iced vodka and guava hitting my tongue. I need it. I'm shoving shit all over the fridge, clearing everything in my wake.

My head was half in the fridge, next to the rotten lettuce I buy to pretend I'm a good person, when I hear the world's longest, wettest burp in the history of burps and it makes me want to vomit.

I pull my head out of the fridge and stare at him, dead on.

Sheep. Of course it was him. Never before in his life had he enjoyed the carbonated goodness of a guava High Noon, but today, of all days, the only day I really wanted one, really needed one, and, quite honestly, it wasn't even my fault, but everyone else's.

I watched with disgust as he dropped the last can of my precious High Noons, sucked dry, into my already-too-full garbage can.

The least he could fucking do is recycle.

CHAPTER 40:

A NEW BREED OF RAT

Jack
Location: Little Gray House
Mood: Distrustful

TYPICAL. FORTY YEARS LATER, AND THINGS HADN'T CHANGED A BIT BETWEEN me and June.

No matter. I have much bigger problems than the problems I left in the nineties. Ha! I'll need to write that one down in my notebook!

First, the FBI. Problem Number One. Clearly. Or was it? Problem Number One may have just been kicked to the curb by a new, more pressing problem. I can feel my ears turn reddish-purple, which tends to happen when I get mad. Cool your jets, Jack. Don't let 'em see you sweat. I wasn't sure if I was referring to the two goons in suits who seemed to be following me everywhere, my ex-wife, or, my new problem, Pete.

Where was that guy, anyway? I reached into the pocket of my Lee work pants, best work pants on the market by far if you ask me, and I felt around for New Problem Number One. I wasn't sure what this was for sure. And I know my son-in-law loves my daughter. But let's face it, these things aren't about love, they're about lust. And lust is a Deadly Sin.

I chew the inside of my cheek as I toss this around in my head, barely aware of the ramblings droning in the background from my ex-wife—some unbelievable Facebook thing or another. I don't know, I don't bother with that garbage so I tune her out.

I excuse myself to the bathroom, being careful to lock the door behind me. Love my grandson, but he has the sonar ability of a bat and was always popping up at the least opportune times. Oh, I wasn't worried about him walking in on me using the bathroom. Oh, no. He's eight now, and he can read. Damn smart, that one is. Sure wish Pete had taken the family name. Joseph would be a good one to continue it. Sure better than that boring, un-Italian name, Cook.

I uncurl and smooth the little scrap of paper on the cool, quartz countertop. No sir, even an eight year old would understand what this was. A love letter. Albeit a short one, but it was addressed to my son-in-law, unless there's another "My darling Peter" (gross) living at this address. Or, unless my daughter has a habit of signing the name "Molly" and an out-of-state phone number when writing her husband letters.

I'm not sure what's going on here, but I'm going to figure this one out. I smell another rat, and it's not of the FBI breed.

CHAPTER 41:

i CAN TAKE CARE OF YOU

Molly

Location: Molly's Thoughts

Mood: Pissed

I HAD A GOLF LESSON THE DAY AFTER I LEFT YOU THE LUNCH I MADE, JUST for you. I'm slightly, okay very, disappointed that you haven't even mentioned it to anyone. I mean, I know I didn't sign my name to the little heart note I included, but surely you knew it was me? It's not like I brought you peanut butter and jelly, Pete, it was sushi! From the best place in town! How many random women bring you lunch, Peter? Is it more than just me and your wife?

Or maybe, you thought your wife dropped it off. I mean, you two barely talk to each other, so how would you know if she did? Does she even care about you enough to drop off a lunch, Peter? Doesn't seem much like it to me, with all the reading and coffee drinking she does. Have you noticed the extra weight on her hips lately? It's probably the coffee calories. I'll keep my figure nice and trim for you. No lumpy baby belly or stretch marks here.

Pathetic. What you and Clarissa have is hardly what I would want in a marriage, but that would never happen to me because I would pay attention to my husband and there is no way on this damn planet that some other bitch would be dropping him off lunch without me knowing. No sir. Wouldn't happen.

Which is exactly what I was thinking about when I walked by your car and bent over to tie my shoe next to your front tire in the golf course parking lot. I know you were watching me. I made sure to pop my ass back a little higher, just for you. I even shook it a little.

And before I stood up, I slapped a magnetic tracker behind your wheel well, because, well, I don't want to lose you, Peter. Your wife? She's kind of boring me. I think about you more, now.

Leroy will be excited.

CHAPTER 42:

THE TOOTH AND THE LITTLE TINY SAUSAGE

Leroy
Location: Little Gray House, Out Front
Mood: Anxious

My phone rings as I'm walking up to the door to the little gray house. It's Molly. Better answer it. "Are you sure you're done with her?" I ask. "That's awfully quick!"

I need to hold myself back. Don't get too excited. Molly might change her mind, just to fuck with me. It was never-ending, this constant pissing-match of a power struggle. But goddamn. I can't help myself. If Molly is done with her it's my turn, before it becomes her turn again (complicated, I know) but I want her. Now. I think about those perfect little tits, like peaches, and how I can't wait to bite them. I like to bite hard, especially pretty little bitches because they scream the most. Like little baby lambs.

I feel my pants start to shift. There was a flutter of . . . what was that? Life?

Was this the bitch who was finally going to get my dick to work?

None of the others had, not for long, anyway. Except that one girl. The last one. The one whose tooth I knocked out while forcing my half-limp cock into her mouth. She was crying, and I don't care about the crying, prefer it, actually, but it made her face look ugly, and how the fuck was I supposed to get a boner with Little Miss Ugly Face?

So, I backhanded her. Right in the face while she had her mouth around my dick. She choked for a minute, gagging and coughing, and before I knew it, I had a teeny, tiny little tooth, laying right on my dick, where it stayed for a minute after she spat it out. And, like the exotic Corpse Flower that blooms so rarely that that's its honest-to-god name, my dick got hard, totally hard, and roared to life.

I click off the call, more excited than a pig in shit, with a raging boner, and ring the doorbell.

CHAPTER 43:

SPYING ON DAD

Clarissa
Location: Little Gray House
Mood: Nosy

My dad has been in the bathroom forever. He's not generally a shit forever at someone else's house guy, that's more my mom's style. I wish he would hurry up. He better not be stinking up my bathroom.

My mom has been forever embarrassing me with her wonky bowels. From friends, to boyfriends, to my husband, they have all been victims of entering the bathroom after June. I still get embarrassed about it, especially when my mom starts her passing-gas games in public. She thinks it's hilarious, because she will just leave the aisle and go to the next one, while I am left, basically dying from suffocation from a deadly combination of rotten eggs and popcorn.

The doorbell rings as I'm escaping the craziness of my living room and trying to spy on my dad. I stub my toe on the door jamb, leaving any chance at staying inconspicuous gone. "Goddamn mother fucking hell!" I mumble-yell as my baby toe starts bleeding all over the oak floors. Usually, I'd be excited about this type of bleeding non-injury, as I would use it as an excuse to put my feet up, binge watch serial killer documentaries, and veg. Every mother reading this can feel my hopes dashed, as I remember my present mess.

"Clarissa! Is that you?" my dad yells. "I can hear you out there, swearing. And taking the Lord's name in vain!"

Damn it. He is way too close to the door to be using the bathroom. I've watched enough true crime to know how to observe people. This stuff is for the rookies. I hope he doesn't ask me what number commandment taking the Lord's name in vain is, because I know it is one, but I've plumb forgotten the number. This is the perfect opportunity for him to quiz me on commandments, knowing full well I will fail, and he isn't taking it. That is exactly how I know my dad is up to something, and I'm going to figure out what it is.

I smudge the extra blood from my toe into the rug, telling myself that I'll deal with that later, knowing full well I won't, and walk to the door to see just how much more fuckery we can add to this day.

CHAPTER 44:

THE HUMAN LIE DETECTOR

Jack

Location: Little Gray House
Mood: Distrustful

I RUN THE WATER AND PUMP SOME SOAP INTO THE SINK. I EVEN FAKE DRY my hands. That daughter of mine is eavesdropping. She must suspect Peter of something. That's why she's so on edge. Maybe she knows about the affair. I shake my head as I fold the towel back up. No way. She would have thrown him out by now, and you know what? I would support her, and so would the Pope! Affairs are grounds for an annulment in the Holy Catholic faith. I should know. I've been trying to get one for more than a quarter of a century.

Well, there's only one way to deal with this. *Mano a mano.* I'll have to make a quick trip out to the golf course while everyone is occupied. I'll ask him right to his face if he's stepping out on my daughter. I'll tell him. I'll say, "You know Pete? You can lie to me, and you can lie to Clarissa. You can lie to anyone you want. But you know who you can't lie to, Pete? God. God knows." And then, I'll look at him, square in the kneecaps. Works like a charm, and perfectly legal. Good old father-in-law intimidation. What? I'm not in the Mafia, I've told you this before. Doesn't mean I haven't seen the same movies everyone else has, does it?

That's what I call my human lie detector test. I'll know. I'll know right when I look him in the eyes and bring up God if he's lying to me.

And with that, I slip out the back door before anyone can notice.

CHAPTER 45:

DEFLATE GATE

Leroy
Location: Little Gray House
Mood: Deflated

I FINALLY GET AN ANSWER AT THE FRONT DOOR AFTER WHAT FEELS LIKE ages. The only good thing, or pitiful thing, I suppose, when you consider how infrequent it is, is that my hard-on is gone. It's kind of more like a deflated balloon, and although I'm sad to see it go, I know how to get it back. You open the door and your mouth is half open, like you were in the middle of saying something. I see your pretty little teeth. Gosh, have I noticed them before? I feel my crotch start to tingle.

"Yes?" You're clearly annoyed. This was a quicker job than most. We have lots going on at one time. Usually we have more time to make people feel comfortable after stalking them for a few months, figuring them out. Comfortable or not, this bitch would have her face in my lap by tomorrow and there wasn't a damn thing she could do about it.

"I've come to collect my trap. Unless you've noticed any mice signs? Shit? Anything like that?"

Her face says she's listening, but I can tell she's not. She doesn't want to let me in, I can tell. But there's company here and she isn't alone, so she feels safe. I can almost see her think.

And she opens the door, and she lets me in.

CHAPTER 46:

HOME STRETCH

Molly

Location: The Cemetery
Mood: Giddy

I GET A TEXT FROM LEROY AS I'M WALKING TO MY CAR AT THE CEMETERY. "I'm in," it reads. Good. I check my phone to make sure Pete's dot hasn't moved. Nope, still at work. Thankfully the cheap tracker I put on his car hadn't fallen off. I've been watching him ever since. His little dot was so cute, moving all around the city. He works too much. If I were his wife, I would make sure he didn't have to. Clarissa really needs to learn how to take care of her husband better.

I always hate to leave my friends. I love coming here. It's so peaceful. Plus, people are always so sympathetic toward me. I come visit often, as much as I can, really, because even though they're dead, they are some of the best friends I ever had. Or wished I had. Like Clarissa, all of these women had something in common, and that is that they weren't up to my standards. For some reason or another. Some I had met and even befriended, and some I had just met from afar, like Clarissa.

I get in my car, or rather, the car I stole from the waitress with that hideous missing tooth, and head for the little gray house on the hill. This car looks so much better green than it did black. The paint job was totally worth the little theft it took to pay for it.

CHAPTER 47:

OVER THE THRESHOLD

Leroy

Location: Little Gary House
Mood: Hot and Horny

I WISH MOLLY WOULD HURRY UP. TIMELINESS IS NOT HER STRONG SUIT. It's so hot in this furnace room, pretending to be getting rid of my one trap that takes an hour to do, apparently. There are a few things that make me angry. Being hungry, being horny, and being hot. My face is dripping with sweat. I don't know how much longer I can last staying in this hotbox.

This little desperate housewife's castle has probably never had so much as an ant, let alone a mouse. No, my sister, Molly, she's crazy, and she sent me here a few months ago. She first saw Clarissa at the school, figured out where she lived, and sprinkled some crumbs around the house. Put the flier for the company I work for in your door, a few fake reviews from neighbors, and, next thing I knew, Peter hired me.

This job has been planned for a long time, but it took forever to execute and get our cameras in this place so Molly could do her favorite thing: Watch. And that bitch thinks I'm crazy. She literally has cameras in anywhere from five to ten people's houses at a time, so that she can swoop into their lives and pretend to be the best friend they've been waiting for. She's the pervert, really, not me.

It was like Fort Knox, trying to penetrate this family. That little pansy really tried to protect her. He built his castle walls up big and strong, but, at the end of the day, it didn't matter. He hired the company I work for, I made sure I got the job, and here we are.

We're like vampires: We don't strike until we're invited in. It's more of a practicality than anything. But taking your prey by surprise usually means forced entry. I'm no dummy and don't want to get caught. So, it's always a sneak attack. Most bad guys don't just walk up behind you like the boogie man, even though that's what people think. No, we're always watching, waiting, trying to find the next vulnerability to exploit. The easier the better. Low-hanging fruit, my favorite. Most people like us prefer random, unknown victims. Way harder to get caught, but this is way more fun and personal, which both Molly and I prefer.

Those teachers never thought I'd amount to anything. And look at me now. Look at how smart I am.

Those bitches were just like all the rest. Stupid. Whores. A walking pussy on legs.

Mine, to do with as I please.

I want nothing more than to barge upstairs and get this show on the road so I can have a little bedtime snack of a suburban housewife's cunt, but I need to wait for Molly. I can't do anything without Molly. She holds some pretty bad shit over my head, so as much as I don't always want to do her bidding, I have to. At least until I can get rid of her. God, won't that be fun.

I hear Molly rapping on the basement window, the one I had unlatched last time I was here. I tiptoe over, push it open, and help her in like a good little brother.

CHAPTER 48:

DON'T GO DOWN THE STAIRS

Clarissa
Location: Little Gray House
Mood: Ominous

MY DAD IS ALL OF A SUDDEN MIA. MY HUSBAND IS STILL AT WORK. THE Feds took off somewhere around the time I stubbed my toe spying on my dad. I don't know where they went. Maybe they finally understand that although my dad is a proud Republican, he's no criminal. He's a good guy, horrid political views or not. I'm sure my dad thinks the same of my views, but that doesn't mean they are illegal, or wrong. Maybe they went back to Quantico, or wherever they're from.

I'm left with Ellen, my mom, and Sheep. Joseph is somewhere in the bowels of the house, probably watching YouTube and sneaking snacks. I wish he was up here to help me out. I contemplate turning off the WiFi to smoke him out, but decide against it.

I have to do something. I need five minutes to think. I shoo the remaining crowd to the upper deck, the one with the no stairs down, and I load them with drinks and snacks. Little tiny taco bites on puff pastry, a gigantic vegetable tray, meat and cheese of every variety, and individual charcuterie cups. I like charcuterie and all, but all those germs? Gross. Do you know how dirty people's hands are? I won't even start. Easy fix, by the way, just do them individually in cups. Way cuter and way cleaner. Ask my mother in law, she's a pro on infection control.

I even gave them some High Noons in a cooler. Not the good ones of course, all of the rejects you have to buy in order to get the good ones. Don't get me wrong, they are all delicious and the only brand I drink, but I prefer what I prefer. However, we have a local store that just started selling them in four-packs of whatever flavor you like. Honest to god. I don't ever drink so this may not be new, but it blew my mind. I can just buy guava? Game changer.

Like most moms, I do my best thinking in the shower. But since that wasn't an option, I did the next best mom dip known to mom: I went to the laundry room to pretend to do laundry. No laundry would be done, a hissy fit might be had, and I might even cry. Whatever. Better than this shit, I think, as I descend the stairs to the basement below.

CHAPTER 49:

JUST A BUCK SHOT AWAY

Jack
Location: The Golf Course Parking Lot
Mood: Demanding

I park Ellen's Honda at the back of the golf course parking lot and take a look at the lay of the land. I don't want Peter to see me coming. I might catch this affair live. Most affairs tend to happen at work. I looked up all the statistics on my way here. I see the pro shop down a hill, less than a buck shot away. Perfect. It looks quiet, should be a good time to sneak up on him.

The door buzzer announces me as I walk in. Dammit, no surprising anyone around these parts. I start to feel homesick for Way Far Away already. Not enough cows or rocks around here.

"Jack!" Pete calls from behind the counter. "Were the ladies driving you nuts?"

"This has nothing to do with the ladies, Peter," I say. Good, he's confused. Perfect. That's another good tactic. Confuse your prey before you pounce.

I unfold the love letter before slamming it on the counter.

Wham!

"Explain this, Peter," I say calmly.

Pete takes a moment to look at the note, acting like he's never seen it before or something. I hate to break it to him, but the love letter is literally addressed to him. Says "Peter," right there at the top.

Once Pete has finished the note, his face turns white.

Good. Little jerk knows he's caught. That's what you get when you fool around on my daughter.

"So," I push. Explain.

"I can't explain, Jack! I really can't. But, listen. I swear to fucking God I would never have an affair. Have you tasted your daughter's cooking? Clarissa has been saying things are off lately and she thought maybe she had a stalker of some sort. Honestly, I haven't paid attention because she talks about this kind of stuff all the time, and sometimes she thinks that everyone is either a drug addict or a serial killer. If I know Clarissa, she's in deep shit and we need to get back there! Like, now!" Peter is already grabbing his keys and walking to the door.

The door buzzer sounds again.

What the fuck? Why, for the love of God, is the FBI back?

CHAPTER 50:

SHE'S A FAINTER!

Clarissa
Location: Little Gray House
Mood: Hungry

I WALK INTO THE LAUNDRY ROOM SO I CAN HAVE SOME PRIVACY TO THINK. Upstairs, I swear I hear the faint click of our new patio door lock, but that's impossible because our guests outside are happily stuffing their faces with all the treats I made them and getting sauced on reject-flavors High Noons. I should have put out some edibles. Nope, illegal, immoral, and I would risk my status as a medical cannabis patient. Erase that thought. I do wish more of my friends would go the appropriate route and get their medical cards, but the price! Outrageous. Hopefully the Ministry of Cannabis works on that. It's just not fair.

I start to think about my options. I should call Peter and tell him to come home. Sometimes I take on way more than I can handle, and I end up crawling back to my husband, confessing my latest disastrous idea. Every time, he pulls me back in his arms and says, "I got you, baby."

But no. I'm not going to bother him. He puts up with so much of my bullshit. I mean, the guy lets me fall asleep next to him watching serial killer documentaries and doesn't complain. And besides, I only have WiFi in the laundry room, the cell service sucks and goes from one bar to none constantly. Just a few more hours until I have my husband home and all of this company gone.

I scroll through social media and roll my eyes at what my mom had posted earlier, while she was here. Some stupid, "How many days old were you when you learned" post, a supposed hack that was super obvious and unknown except to the people lucky enough to see these memes on social media. Usually, they don't actually work. No matter how many times I fact-checked these posts for my mom, she continued to come up with more, increasingly outrageous, every time. From how to clean the inside of your oven door, to how to stop a boil over with a wooden spoon, to today's gem: "I was today years old when I learned that the middle part of the Oreo container is actually for salsa." What the fuck? Go look at your Oreo container right now. Right there down the middle. It must be true! It was on social media, of course it is! Oh my gosh! It's for salsa. Ha! I'm so lucky I saw this post so I, too, can enjoy Oreos and salsa. What the fuck?

I turn to head back upstairs, but the laundry room door is shut. I told you things were just getting weird. I hear laughter. I recognize it. Kind of? Wait . . . is that two people laughing? I listen closer, using a cup I pick up from the floor to amplify the sound. Write that down for your personal *How to Survive a Serial Killer or Other Nefarious Situations* notebook. I have one and you should, too. Using what you have and listening are key. It helps if the people you live with are slobs so you have extra cups laying around.

There are two people standing outside the laundry room door. I'm not so sure I want to find out who they are, because I think I might know and it is not good. Not good at all.

I look back at the only window in the room, if you can call it that. Typical walk-out ranch with egressless windows that don't even open. That won't be any help. I haven't been able to fit through a space that size since I was in tenth grade and being harassed about my weight by my boyfriend. Honest to God. He told me he would dump me if I gained any weight. Loser. I'm going to get some Oreos when I get out of here. A family-sized pack of extra-lardy double-stuffed. Pete has absolutely no problem with my fluffy mom bottom, and I think he actually even prefers it! A prize, that one. I need to live. I can't ever be that lucky again, even in a brand new life. If I end up a ghost after this, I decide, I'm going to haunt him so he can't get another girlfriend. Or wife. And if haunting is too much for him, I'll at least eat crackers on his side of the bed so he knows I've been there. Wait, can ghosts eat crackers? Or lay down?

The door opens, and I decide, in that moment, that this is my time to shine.

For some reason, with all my late night documentary watching, true-crime reading, and the events of late, I know that I am face to face with two, real, live, active serial killers, not just one. Lord, why couldn't they be the dormant type?

And before I can channel my inner Clarise, or even Diane, my vision starts to blur and, all of a sudden, everything goes black. Just like that time in college when I donated too much plasma in a week.

I know where this is going. With that final thought I, quite dramatically, faint on my laundry room floor.

CHAPTER 51:

GET THE TARP

Molly
Location: Little Gray House
Mood: Argumentative

"WELL, THAT WAS EASIER THAN EXPECTED!" I GIGGLED. "HAVE WE EVER had one faint before, Leroy?"

He grins. "Not that quick, sis. A new record, for sure."

"We don't have long, Leroy!" I chide. "Better get your sick sexual–sadist business done."

"It's a little different having an audience, Molly."

"Well, that's where we are, loser, so you have, I don't know, five minutes? Do your disgusting thing, pretend she's your girlfriend and actually likes you . . . What? You think I don't know? You disgust me. You probably can't even get it up in five minutes, so you might be shit out of luck and miss out on your perfect little Clarissa."

"You're just jealous that she's prettier than you. And you think you're so much better than me. You're the real sicko. Stalking people and watching them like you do," Leroy snarls.

"Oh. So you think getting off on other people's pain is less sick than watching some cameras? And, she's definitely not prettier than me. Ask her husband."

"Can we argue about who's more fucked up and prettier some other time?"

"No. I'm so sick of you. I honestly don't know why I haven't killed you yet. You know why you are the sickest? Because I know you think about Mom every time you get a chance with a girl. I've heard you. That's why no woman who has a choice wants anything to do with you. So you have to force it, or no sex for you. You have mommy issues, Leroy. And you're fucked up and your dick doesn't work and you're worthless and so is your dick. Which is also pretty tiny, by the way."

Leroy

THAT BITCH. I'M FUMING. I TURN AROUND AND BACKHAND HER. THE BLOW knocks her over and she grunts, holding her mouth.

"What the actual fuck, Leroy?" Molly was spitting blood all over the linoleum. So much for a clean crime scene. I spot a tarp in the corner and drag it out, preparing the floor. Megan might be dumb enough to leave her DNA all over this place, but I sure the fuck ain't. And I have lots of DNA to spray.

CHAPTER 52:

SHEET CAKES AND ANOTHER TOOTH

Leroy
Location: Little Gray House – The Laundry Room
Mood: Gross

"Ugh. You're so gross, Leroy." Molly makes a face as I fan Clarissa's pretty blonde hair out around her. It looks like my mom's. She looks like an angel, even though she's definitely not dead, just fainted. For now.

Normally Molly tosses me her friend rejects to fuck and then get rid of after she offs them. Her cast offs, her not good enoughs. And finally, after I've done nothing but her dirty work for two whole years, helping her kill broads and disposing of their bodies anytime she so much as asked, she is rushing me? I even killed our bitch mom because she told me to. I do feel bad about that. I'm going to have nightmares about it, but I will never tell Molly that because she'll call me a sissy.

I couldn't bear to use our usual methods. *We are blunt force trauma fans—easy, hard to trace, up close and personal, but messy, requiring a tarp.* So, I pussed out. I probably made it worse for her in the end. Starved the bitch for a couple of days and poisoned her with carbon monoxide before I left this morning. Her brains were cooked, scrambled eggs before I took my morning shit.

That's what my nightmare will be. I shiver. My eighty-five-year-old mother, dead in the back of her '93 Buick Regal, with dusty blue velvet seats. I locked the car door before I left just in case the old bird woke up. Didn't want her to escape. And Molly doesn't think I'm smart.

I look at Clarissa, my angel, laying on the laundry room floor. Waiting for me. Spread out like a fucking sheet cake for the taking. Yummy, yummy, what flavor do I get today? I'm reaching for her blouse and licking my chops. God, I can't wait to pull that blouse down and see those peaches! I've waited so long, I deserve this! I see a flash of my mom in the back seat of her car, maggots coming out of her eye sockets, and her skeleton hand outstretched, stiff, and bouncing gently with the creak of her bones.

Immediately, I lose the half-ass erection I do have. I backhand Clarissa, right in the face. A little blood starts trickling out of her mouth and nose. She looks hot, like that girl on *Pulp Fiction*. She groans, still unconscious.

Then she spit out a pretty little tooth on the tarp, and I'm ready.

CHAPTER 53:

SCAR JO

Clarissa
Location: Little Gray House
Mood: Wistful

I'm not sure what's going on or where I am, but something stinks. Like dirty feet and rat piss. I taste something metallic and move my tongue around my mouth to assess the damage. Ugh. Missing a tooth. I know this isn't the time to be vain, but Lord, if you are listening, if you let a serial killer kill me, of all people, serial-killer obsessed me, at least let me keep my teeth. Well, the rest of them, anyway.

I realize I'm losing focus. Why am I praying about my teeth when there are literally two serial killers in my house and I have no clue where my child is? My little Corn Dog. He's been asking me to call him that lately, because he loves hand-dipped corn dogs so much. I pray again, this time for his safety, See, good mom! Even in the face of danger! I can get veneers, I decide. Much prettier teeth, anyway. I shudder at the thought of the process. I watched a video one time, and they shave some of your real teeth down to tiny little stubbins, like shark teeth. No matter. Whatever I have to do.

I force myself not to move. Play dead. Always play dead, unless you're dealing with a necrophiliac. In that case, playing dead would be a very poor choice. They prefer dead bodies to live ones. Fucking gross. I sure hope these two are some other type of serial killer monster. Shit, I'll even trade a necrophiliac for a sexual sadist, and if you've ever heard of Ted Bundy or John Wayne Gacy, you will understand the horrible predicament I'm in and it isn't even noon.

That's it, I decide. I'm playing dead, I'm going to buy myself time, and I for sure am not letting them take me to any sort of second location. That would for sure mean death. I hear my dad in my ear. *"Remember, Clarissa, girl. God gave you two ears and one mouth for a reason."* Thanks, Dad. Time to listen and assess my predator. Just like you taught me how to do, all those years ago in the deer stand. "Wait longer than you think, babycakes," he would whisper, until I finally got used to the feel and pressure of the gun.

With that tip, I blew the next deer's head off, and I'm going to do the same thing to these losers. What the fuck is the singular possessive form of deer? I'm not actually a writer. An editor will have to work that out.

Who am I kidding? I don't own a gun. I grew up with guns, sure, I even went to Firearm Safety class, and if you don't believe me look at the back of my drivers' license. Says it right on it. Where I grew up, Way Far Away, it was a required class for all twelve-year-olds. Right alongside D.A.R.E, one of the country's responses to the war on drugs, and Family Life. I brought my egg baby twins to gun class, Gabrielle and Mackenzie. I didn't do so well parenting them, I returned them cracked and stinky after my week with them, but I did ace my firearms safety test. Nailed every target right in the middle. And, being funny even way back then, I would blow the invisible steam off my twenty-two, the one with a timberwolf carved in the stock.

Anyway, in this great state of Minnesota, you aren't allowed to own a gun if you are a patient of medical cannabis. Oh no. Don't want the hippies getting too trigger happy, I guess. I should write a letter about that, too, I think. Although I wouldn't even own a gun, personally, knowing all the facts I know about how often they are more likely to be used against you instead of helping you, and I can't even kill a butterfly, so what do I think I am going to do with a gun? No, enter my house and you will meet my taser and a nine iron. Much more effective. Plus, the alarm would have called the police before you stepped foot in my house, so don't try it. I may have gotten a gun by then, anyway, after I write this scathing letter I have planned about how I was unable to defend myself in my own home, due to needing some weed to stay less triggered.

God, I hope I can make it out of this alive so I can write a book of my real-life adventure with two serial killers. Lord knows I have read every thriller, true crime, and dark comedy book known to humans. Eat your heart out, Diane Sawyer, I think. This is real reporting, right here. Never been done before, pretty sure.

I need to relax. So, I close my eyes and meditate on who I want to play me in the movie version of the book I hope to write if I live. After I get veneers, of course. Can't be going to a movie premiere missing a tooth! I almost laugh, but remember where I am and get back to meditating. I don't have to think hard at all about who would be me, I have known this answer since I started writing this book in my head three days ago.

I smile and breathe.

CHAPTER 54:

THREE HOTS AND A COT

Jack
Location: The Golf Course
Mood: Tired

As soon as the Feds walked in, I have to admit that I was so over this day. I turned around, put my hands behind my back and said, "Take me away, Rat-Face!" Everyone stared at me, and I can't believe they're so surprised I would voluntarily go to jail. Hey, three hots and a cot, haha, isn't that the lingo? See? I could fit right in and have a nice little vacation, away from this mess, and some jail cookies my daughter told me about. Supposed to have tons of nutrition, right in a little oatmeal cookie that has the consistency and look of a hockey puck. Sounds divine!

Hey, I pay my taxes, and other people's too. They even have church services in jail, so I won't be missing out on any services. I'll have to double check that I can get approved for a furlough to attend Adoration. I do have a triple slot this week to be responsible for.

"Mr. Macellaio please take your hands out from behind your back. You are not under arrest!" Rat-Face orders.

"Take me to your leader!" I exclaim. "I want to see the manager! Take me to jail! Directly to jail! I will not pass go! I will not collect $200!"

"Listen to us. We'll explain later, but we have reason to believe that your daughter is in trouble," Baldy interjects.

"The Democrat or the Republican?"

Both Feds look shocked.

"The true Catholic, or the one that's the Santas and Bunnies sort?"

They are still just staring at me, goddamn mouths on the floor.

What? I was just curious.

CHAPTER 55:

MRS. MOLLY COOK

Molly

Location: The Little Gray House

Mood: Impatient

I can't stand to be around my brother. He's so desperate. So vile. I can totally understand why normal girls want nothing to do with him. That's why I pass him my rejects, the ones that aren't up to my friend standards. Obviously, I have pretty high ones. Keeps him away from me, too. Gross.

I know Leroy thinks I'm a loser right back, and I don't care. I watch what he does to those girls before I kill them—he's way too soft for that!—and I remember what he used to do to me when I was a little girl. He took advantage of me when I needed him most, pretending to protect me from our monster dad, when he was almost as bad as him already, at age eight. I run my tongue over the missing tooth in the back. Leroy's work, of course. Weird fucker has a thing for teeth, and I've never figured out why. Regardless, he's a pervert, a loser, and he will rot in hell someday.

He sure is taking his sweet time with this one. He keeps stopping and stroking her hair, like she's a goddamn baby doll, not some full grown woman he has been fantasizing about sexually violating for the last two weeks straight.

I look down at her, kind of sad that we can't be besties like I truly wanted, but kind of excited for what's to come. I need to find something in this shithole to kill her with. Something I can crack her over her pretty little head with. I'll make sure I hit her on the back of the head so the egotistical bitch can have an open casket. I'll also make sure to bring her husband my best hotdish to comfort him.

I'm thinking about Peter and how happy he is going to be. I've come to the conclusion that he was sick of her too. How couldn't he be? He just didn't know how to fix the problem, so here I come and fix all of his problems with one swift crack. I pick up an ugly, thick, golden candlestick from a shelf. I give it a couple solid whacks against the cement floor to make sure it will hold up. Perfect. Not a dent on it. Back to Peter.

Mrs. Molly Cook?

Sure does have a nice ring to it.

CHAPTER 56:

LiGHTBAR♀, ♀iREN♀, AND AiRHORN♀

Jack

Location: In the FBI Truck

Mood: Prayerful

"OH LORD, PLEASE LET MY BABYCAKES BE SAFE! I'LL EVEN STOP HARASSING her about prayer in school!"

She's a firecracker, that one. Born too early, born too sick, but she was a fighter. Damn right. Just like I raised her.

Tears well up in my eyes. I turn to Rat-Face and Baldy and say, "Step on it, boys! It's time to save my daughter!"

And before they could stop me, I flipped the lightbar and sirens on, rolled the window down, grabbed an airhorn, and yelled "Babycakes! I'm coming for you! And I'm bringing the whole FBI, just like you'd want!"

I can't believe it. My little serial-killer nut has gotten herself in quite the pickle. She's always been too nice to everyone. And people could feel it in her too, they could. Would come and sit down and tell her their whole life story on a 5:00 a.m. train, didn't even know her from Adam! This couldn't be how our story ended. Over my dead body. I am not going to bury my baby.

And as soon as that FBI truck pulls up remotely close to my daughter's little gray house on the hill, I jump out the window, diabetes and gout be damned, and run through that front door to save the day. I mean, my daughter.

I wish I had packed my Indiana Jones hat.

CHAPTER 57:

THE BURRITO

Leroy

Location: Little Gray House, the Laundry Room
Mood: Rushed

I AM SO TIRED. THIS IS THE LONGEST WEEK EVER. I TRY TO GET MY ERECTION back, but all I can think of is maggots and my mom.

Wait. What is that noise?

I look at Molly.

She heard it too.

And in one shake of a lamb's tail, I roll Clarissa up like a burrito, in her own tarp, in her own laundry room, and prepare for the shitstorm to come.

CHAPTER 57:

PRAYERS FROM THE FOXHOLE

Jack
Location: Little Gray House
Mood: Faithful

I HAVEN'T RUN THAT FAST SINCE BACK WHEN I WAS A KID AND HAD TO GET home before dark lest I get my ass whooped. Chased with a wooden spoon by my tiny spitfire of a mother is a little more accurate, but I'm Italian and I can tend to exaggerate. She was small, Italian, and fierce. I smile. I can't help but think there's quite a bit of mom in my daughter.

I stop to say another quick prayer and yes, of course I'm in a hurry. Quite a hurry! Rat-Face and Baldy told me and Pete that the exterminator Pete hired to take care of their mouse problem was thought to be responsible for four other deaths in the past two years! Right here in this town! With all the research Clarissa says she does on serial killers and psychopaths, she must not be as talented as she thinks. Why can't this kid just use her degree? I don't even care that it's from a state school.

So yes, I understand the urgency. But, in times of crisis, we pray first. Because just like my dad before me used to say, "Jack, if you don't believe in God before you go to war, you will be sure to meet him in the foxhole."

This was my foxhole today.

This was my war.

So I stopped, and I prayed.

CHAPTER 58:

THE CRAZY HYENA

Clarissa
Location: Little Gray House
Mood: Delirious

MY ZEN-LIKE MEDITATION SESSION OF SCARLETT JOHANSSON PLAYING ME and collecting all the awards was rudely interrupted by my present reality.

Well put guacamole on me, I'm a burrito! Corndog would get it, and he would laugh. He would probably sprinkle me with cheese, too. My eyes well up at the thought of him. It's too much. Must concentrate. Block it out. Compartmentalize. Must survive. One good decision I've made today is not to cut the WiFi. Hopefully he's holed up somewhere playing *Rainbow Friends,* without a care in the world.

Your brain does crazy things when you think you're going to die. I now know this to be true. I mean, I really know now. It's the start of a new awful joke. So, I was in a room, with two deranged serial killers, rolled up like a giant burrito in a tarp! God, I have my dad's horrible sense of humor.

I don't even care if the book that I might write gets made into a movie anymore, I think. Nope, I'd even take a straight-to-streaming movie, which is the bottom of the barrel. I wonder about the self-published route. I wish

I had written a will. For what? My debt? Plus, if I make it through, I will be the best wife ever and give my husband a hall pass with a starlet like in that movie, cleverly named *Hall Pass*. Ha!

 No offense to my husband, but I think Scar Jo is a little out of his reach. Literally she is super tall and he is not super tall. Maybe Erica Jayne from the *Housewives* will be available, I think. She might need money after the divorce. No, she would scare him and she's also like eight feet tall. What is with all of these tall women? I missed out on that gene. Hopefully in the next life I can grow a few inches.

Maybe I'll have to take someone trying to make their move from music to acting, like a Lindsay Lohan type. No, she's not right. Maybe Jessica Simpson? I love her, and I'd love to think we look basically identically in a pair of daisy dukes. Oh god, I'm getting delirious. Miley Cyrus is probably more realistically like me, and I love her voice.

Maybe laughing will make dying hurt less, I think. I cry–snort, because I'm scared now. I have definitely pissed my pants at least twice now. I know what's happening here. My brain is shutting down, it knows a bad situation when it sees it. It's protecting itself, making me think of stupid shit like Erica Jayne fucking my husband. At this rate, if I make it out of this mess, I will have dissociated to Mars and my brain will be useless, a glob of Lunch Lady's Mystery Choice hotdish like they used to serve at Catholic school on Tuesday. I gag.

I thought that I knew everything about serial killers, including how to spot and escape them, and here I am. One of my old bosses always says everyone on this planet has a talent. The talent, he told me when he first hired me, is something that you are the 1 percent of. So he always asks people, "What's the talent that you're better than 99 percent of people at?"

And people say all sorts of things. Some say sports, basketball, football, lots of hockey buffs, here in Minnesota. Especially where I grew up, hockeytown USA, I think. Oh no? Is my life flashing before my eyes? I wait. Nope.

Just thinking about hockey. You have to know when to recognize a true sign and when something is a red herring. That was a red herring. I would know.

Anyway, other people say they're artistic, they're an excellent jumper, or that they have the best tater tot casserole in their entire family. What do you think I said? I looked right at him, well, up at him because he's super tall, and I'm super short, and I said, "My top 1 percent skill is that I can recognize when anyone gets a haircut without them telling me. Doesn't matter if it is one-tenth of a millimeter or if they're wearing a hat. I'll see it and I'll notice." That's true, by the way, ask my old coworkers. But, I was lying. I actually have two 1 percent skills, and I'm really not trying to brag, but I'm dying so I may as well.

My other 1 percent skill is identifying serial killers and other psychopaths in general. Of course, I didn't tell him that. I am also excellent at interviewing and I know that you definitely should not say that in an interview. Even if he was cool with it, HR would not be. And now look at me. Locked up with two of them. In my own house. I can't help it anymore. The tears are coming and they won't stop.

I feel my burrito wrapper move and I'm scared to look. I keep my eyes closed as tight as I can and I start laughing because, well, it's quite funny, although morbidly, the predicament I've ended up in. And I think, *I am going to die so you should try that laughing bit in case it works and ends up hurting less.*

And I do. I laugh like a crazy fucking hyena. I laugh so hard I'm crying, snorting, and peeing my pants with whatever is left in my tiny bladder.

I wasn't faking it, either. Because when he peeked over the corner of my tarp burrito, I noticed something. I hadn't noticed it before, because I was exercising my other 1 percent skill—identifying serial killers—and if you don't have more than one of these skills, you wouldn't know, but you can't use two at one time. Unfortunately.

Looks like the dirty old pest guy has gotten a haircut since I saw him last! And I can hardly even type this—and now you know I made it out alive, because you're reading my book. This isn't *Misery* and Kathy Bates doesn't have me locked up, forcing me to write a book. I wish, but no. It's not winter, and there is no snowstorm. I think that ending would be more believable than this.

He didn't have any old haircut. No way, not this psycho. It looked totally normal from the front, but I was more looking at him from an angle, and guess what I saw? No! Not a mullet. They aren't funny enough to make me laugh that hard. No. A rat tale. A braided one. With a tiny neon green elastic band securing the scraggly ends at the bottom of the tail. Looked like a braces band to me, like the ones that my older sister had in fifth grade when she had braces that always snapped. I feel bad now because I used to laugh. *Snap! Ouch! Haha! Mom! Clarissa's laughing at me again!*

What a dumbass! This guy doesn't even know those are horrible for your hair.

And guess what happened? The dirty old pest guy backed away from me and my burrito shell, terrified.

Molly, ever the control freak that she was, couldn't believe that her plans have been derailed. I could see it in the confusion on her face. She's standing there, dumbstruck, kind of like a shell version of herself. Which, by the way, is how I think of psychopaths. They look like us, they walk like us, they might even be prettier, or smarter, and for sure more charming than us. They actually have the same traits as you and me, but they are either way too overdeveloped or underdeveloped. But, there's also something missing. And I know a lot of very important people have studied this and I am really dumbing this down for myself, but, from what I think, I can always tell when I look them in the eye. Windows to the soul and all that. Honestly, can you look into any serial killer's eyes and think they look normal? Try it sometime. Just turn on any Netflix documentary and look at their eyes. So creepy. Pretty soon Richard Ramirez's *Night Stalker* eyes are everywhere on my laundry room wall. Following me, laughing at me, stalking me. Oh my god. I'm hallucinating. Did someone slip me LSD? Stop it. This isn't the seventies and no one has drugged you. *Fuck you, Ramirez, you're dead and you don't scare me. Take those creepy eyes and get out of my house.* I blink. They're gone. Much better.

I hate when people say serial killers can't feel emotion. Yes they can! I just know it, from all of my viewings of them on TV and the two I've met in real life. If you don't believe me, ask the FBI Behavioral Unit, they know too! I've heard they work very deep in the basement, though, so they might be tough to find. If I have a contact after this I'll update my bio. I've suspected plenty of people in my days of being psychopaths. Check out episode seventeen on *Signs of a Psychopath*. That one gets all into it.

Molly was definitely feeling emotion now. The thing is, though, that it was an emotion for herself. She cares quite a lot right now that she didn't get her way. She cares quite even more that she's going to get caught and she isn't going to have friends anymore or a life or fake nails or the ability to play God. She's throwing a hissy fit, actually. Throwing shit around my laundry room! God, there goes the litter box full of cat shit! And my laundry! *There you go, Molly!* I think. Show your undeveloped little prefrontal cortex with all of your toddler tendencies in your big grown-up body! A full-on, adult temper tantrum! What is that in her hand? Is that the candlestick from mom and dad? No way this is ending like that. What is this, *Clue*?

And I let them rage and destroy my laundry room. This is either attention-seeking behavior or psychosis, and the best way to deal with either in this situation seems to be not to pay it any mind. Worked on Corndog's tantrums, and some of them were pretty messy. As I wait, I daydream about the time I carried him out of a birthday party like a surfboard for misbehaving. One of my best mom moments yet. It's totally looking like I will be able to replace the laundry soon enough, with the book and movie deal I imagine I'll be getting for surviving this. Maybe I can finally move the washing machine and dryer next to each other, instead of having them twenty feet apart like they are now. Wouldn't that be nice?

I wasn't sure who would come to save me, but I knew someone would, because even if I don't have a lot of friends, the ones I do have care an awful lot about me. And I'm a phone talker. Annie and Shelby hadn't heard from me for a couple hours, and they should be starting to wonder. Once it hits three, they'll probably send in the big guns with a door rammer. Or, once Mom and Sheep run out of High Noons they'll start searching the place for more. Here's another one for your notebook: Have more than one backup plan. As you can see, I clearly have multiple.

I keep laughing, thinking of the pickle I'm in. Here I am, about to be killed with a candlestick in the laundry room by 2 serial killers like this is *Clue*! And before that I was wrapped up in a burrito. Maybe I am having a mental breakdown. There is no way this is reality. I haven't heard of many people randomly needing anti-psychotic meds in their forties with no prior history, but I always have been an outlier!

Oh, wait, I hear what sounds like the cops upstairs! Yes! It's them! Just like in the movies! Wait, it isn't even just the cops! It's the FBI! This is the best present I have literally ever been given. I mean being alive is number one, I guess, but this is number two. The real FBI! Here to save me from two serial killers! I can't wait to see their reaction. Bet they will be pretty happy to see that they can clear up a bunch of cold cases today, before dinner!

I can hear yelling, "It's the FBI! Come out with your hands up! Leroy! Molly! We know you are in there and we know what you have done! You better come out or we are coming in with our robots and automatic guns! And Clarissa, you are not an FBI agent, you are actually too old to be one, so please just listen and don't do anything unless we tell you to!"

Shit. I can't be saved by an automatic weapon! I don't believe in them and want them banned yesterday. And now I'm benched? Being lectured over a bullhorn by the same FBI who couldn't catch these two idiots? They are really going to tell me what to do?

Ughhhh!

Fine, I'll allow myself to be saved by an automatic weapon, because I really want to live to see this through as I never finish anything. I'll work on writing the legislators (again) tomorrow, after I draft my book. And I'll shut up and listen to the professionals because, like my dad says, God gave me two ears and one mouth for a reason. I'm getting better at knowing when to exercise that one, and it's proven super helpful today.

And before I can think about whether I will allow it anymore, the FBI, well two of the midwest agents anyway, bust into my laundry room, with my dad flying over their shoulders and beating them to me. He takes one look at me and knows I'm totally fine, so he gets right to work, securing the predators. He takes Leroy down first, which is pretty easy, considering he was curled up in the fetal position, with his penis limp in his hands, mumbling nonsensical stuff. I saw my dad take the opportunity to give him a quick whack to the knees with the gun he was holding, and I could hardly blame him. Next, he took one look at Molly and they had a stare-down. He obviously beat her and, when she wasn't paying attention he jumped at her, tackling her at the waist and handcuffing her, with handcuffs he pulled off of his belt loop.

"Always wanted to use these, boys! Bought them on a family trip to California! Got them at a magic shop in Hollywood, the package said they are impossible to get out of! Now, I have lost the key, but I'm sure we can cut them off later. I can help you with that if needed. Don't worry, darlin', I'll only knick ya a few times."

The Feds had their jaws, once again, on the floor. They grabbed Molly and Leroy, whisking them up my stairs and out of my house faster than they had arrived.

Pete took me in his arms and said, "Oh, Clarissa. I can't wait to hear this story. I love you so much, you little weirdo."

And that, my friends, is exactly how I beat two serial killers in the same day, and proved to my dad that I wasn't his little girl anymore, that I could stand on my own, and, most importantly, that I actually heard all of the lessons he taught me all along.

EPILOGUE:

FiVE YEARS, MiNUS TWO WEEKS, LATER

Leroy: Leroy landed himself a nice, lifelong stay at a state supermax facility for the four murders he was convicted of, among many other charges. Everyone hates him, because he's mean and nasty and he stinks. He spends most of his days in the hole, because if there is one thing that prisoners don't like it's people who hurt kids. Well, dumb old Leroy told his cellmate on the very first day that he used to perp on his older sister. He's mostly sad he doesn't have his Mountain Dew and trinket collection anymore. He never killed anyone, not even his mom, it turns out. He kept his trinkets for other reasons. Leroy felt like he was in a relationship with these poor victims—disgusting, I know. All of the jewelry was returned to the victims' families, as it should be. Thankfully, he never got any jewelry from me, and I'm happy to report that Leroy died a virgin. Leroy was a failure in all things, from sex to actually being a real serial killer.

Molly: Unfortunately, although Molly committed the four murders, they can only tie her up on a few wimpy charges because, of course, Leroy covered for her. She will be released in just two weeks, ready to find another corn cob to glob on to. Megan hates that Leroy gets all of the credit for her crimes. She considered fessing up, but since she is getting out soon, she was worried about how that would affect her social status and future friendships. According to Molly, she loves jail and is the most popular gal on her cell block. Upon her release, she plans to move to central Florida and become a life coach.

Marge: Thankfully, Marge isn't dead. She lived to fulfill her dream of making sure her two wicked children didn't inherit her life insurance policy. The police found her back at her home, in the house watching *Jeopardy* and eating popcorn. Leroy thought she couldn't get out of a locked car, but alas, forgot that all cars pretty much can unlock from the inside. Marge wants everyone to know that she still believes her children are idiots. She has moved to a retirement home in California where she mixes up her days with Jazzercise, water yoga, and mocktails. And...she has a boyfriend.

Rat-Face: This case proved to be too much for old Rat-Face, and he retired soon after it was closed. He happened upon a new opportunity, a varmint control company. Actually you might remember it, Splinter-O'Neil Extermination was for sale, and he thought he would be a top-notch rat exterminator.

Sheep and June: Meanwhile, over in Louisiana, Sheep and June decided that living off the grid wasn't for them anymore, fortunately. Unfortunately, they now live in a commune of houseboats in Louisiana, but I'm glad they are enjoying retirement and drinking (their own) High Noons.

Jack and Ellen: Dad went on to win a major award. Just like in our favorite Christmas movie. It wasn't a leg lamp, unfortunately. It was, instead, a beautiful plaque commending him for his bravery that day at my house. Oh, and the FBI? They cleared him. Thank God. Apparently my dad has a doppelganger who was at the Capitol on January 6 and Rat-Face and Baldy are finally out of his life. Except, oddly enough, my dad still runs into Baldy every year at the wild rice processor. They use the same one. Crazy.

Pete: Pete continued being the best husband in the entire world, more in love with his wife than ever. He does wish she would tone down the serial killer habit, unless this does, in fact, earn him a hall pass with a starlet. Just a date. He's a gentleman, and have you met his father-in-law?

Joseph/Corndog: Joseph no longer goes by Corndog, he goes by Hacker. He saw nothing that day, and claims it was one of the best days of his life.

Clarissa: I know, I know. A disappointment. So good, you're thinking, until the ending. But, that's where you're wrong, and clearly I know way more about serial killers than you. Let me explain.

Although all serial killers are different, they can be divided and separated further into groups and subcategories based on their goulish traits and darkest desires. It's also a spectrum, so some people are like super psychopaths and others are less, I don't know, psycho? There's a difference in intensity.

I wouldn't recommend befriending either unless you are a trained professional like me, but you get what I mean. They all do share one trait in common though, at least the ones I've read about, anyway. And the two I have now personally met. They lack social skills. Why? Because they don't have empathy, so they lack insight into behavior, theirs or others. So, they are master copycats. They learn, over time, how to react, the way normal, non-serial killers' would. So while they might do okay in normal, known, practiced situations, they struggle with the random, unknown situations. You following me?

I'm sure they don't teach the laughing-hyena trick over at the FBI or police academy, but they should. Dealing with serial killers, it's a mix of art and science. The science is, they don't do well with random unknown situations. The art is deciding to laugh like a mother-fucking lunatic to disarm their confidence. Why? It isn't normal, and it definitely isn't expected. It confuses their little psycho brain and can buy you three to five seconds. And guess what? It worked. So laugh all you want. But, I do now hold the world record for surviving the most serial killers in one day.

So, there you have it. I'm sorry I lied, but I'm really not, because, thanks to me, two bad people are in jail and absolutely no one was hurt during my sting operation. All of those poor families finally have closure. Personally, I think I should get an award, too, but apparently, the FBI doesn't look too kindly on housewives baiting serial killers, so they wanted that part of the story to disappear.

I really got a lot done this week, which is always how I decide my value. Unhealthy, I know, but honest. This has all happened in the course of five days, from the day the FBI showed up on my dad's doorstep to this moment right now, as I type these final words. And so with that, dear readers, I'll leave you with this:

With gratitude for all your reading, I thank you. And I'll see you right back here on the pages of my next book, very soon! (Borrowed from Diane Sawyer's final send off on ABC NEWS)

Oh my gosh. My phone just rang. Sorry, thought we were done here. Remember how Molly is set to be released next week? She served two-thirds of her sentence, typical in Minnesota, especially for so-called non-violent offenders, which, crazily enough, is how Molly is classified, thanks to her plea deal. The phone number is from a crazy spoof line, I know what this is. It's from a jail or prison, but by the time my phone is ringing, it is virtually untraceable, passing through a bunch of numbers before it comes to mine. Anyway, let me answer this quick,

"Hello?"

(Heavy breathing on the other line)

Faraway sounding voice "Well . . . Clarissa? Have the lambs stopped screaming?"

I drop the phone.

CONFESSION:

LIES OF OMISSION

YOU'RE STILL MAD, I KNOW. I WOULD BE TOO WITH ALL THE BOOKS I READ if that was really the end! I should probably tell you just a couple more secrets. I should tell my dad too, but sometimes, a lie of omission is best.

I sent the photo to the FBI, okay? Yeah. Let me explain.

But first we have to back up. To that day when my husband hired SON Exterminators. God, horrid name. I hope Rat-Face changes that. I do remember that now. I forgot that we ended up hiring him, so that was a plot twist even for me, but when he was talking to my husband that day, I saw her. Right there in the rat truck. And I knew it was weird for some girl I had seen at my kid's school to be doing a ride along with the exterminator.

Yeah, bitch. I saw you first.

I purposely sat by you that day at school.

I knew you were in my house after you took my lighter. I noticed a key was missing. It was the key that turned up in your pervert brother's box of trinkets. He must have taken it when he was here. I have an attached garage. I didn't notice. I have used a house key maybe once in the last decade. A weakness I didn't even know I had. You can gauran-fucken-tee that the key is safely strapped to my inner thigh now. No one's getting it unless they're my husband!

That's why I tested you with the picture of my friend Laura and me. I knew you'd take it. I knew you would instantly hate her and hate that she was in a picture with me when you weren't.

My favorite was when you rolled into my favorite places: My barista? My mother-fucking husband? You didn't even go to the right coffee location. There are four in town, and I love three of them. The one you went to? Way too much milk in their lattes. You have to ask for an extra shot. And my barista? She wouldn't ever be rude, not even to a psycho like you!

Trying to have what I have, trying to take everything I've worked so hard for. Over my dead body. I have prepared for this moment since I was eight years old and first learned what a serial killer was.

When I saw you in the work van, I knew something was up. So, I did what any other good mom would do, and I looked you up. I looked up your social media (whacko!), I looked up your criminal history (pretty boring), and I looked up your relatives. Bingo! I also checked with the company on rules about ridealongs, and those are definitely not a thing.

I visited your poor mom when Leroy was at work one day, and she told me everything. She showed me his sick box of trinkets and, being the true crime junkie that I am, I recognized them right away, plus my house, key, duh. That's when I anonymously sent the picture of my dad to the FBI, because hello, I would need backup. I know my dad like the back of my hand and I knew the first thing he would do is go visit family. so I lured him into fleeing right to my house. I didn't expect it all to happen so fast, or even at all for that matter.

Why not call the police, you ask? I've asked myself that so many times, and the only semi-reasonable explanation that I have is this: One day, not too many years ago, there was a little girl who caught the true-crime bug, and got hooked. She dreamed of being Diane Sawyer and, later, Agent Clarise

Starling. And, I couldn't help myself. I wanted to catch them myself. I'm sorry Rat-Face, Baldy, Quantico, and the FBI.

And while I'm at it, I'm sorry, Dad, for the foul language and sex, but serial killers are ferocious beasts and some emphasis and detail are needed.

Oh, and Molly? The note I dropped that day with the kind words? I already knew who you were from your mom. I did write those words about you. But only for pretend. I didn't mean a word of them.